To Sister: ∩
your encouragement over the
years, With much love,
Carol Ann

MW01043529

A Branch
for
Cass

PK Adams

PublishAmerica
Baltimore

First printing

ISBN: 1-4137-9099-2
PUBLISHED BY PUBLISHAMERICA, LLLP
www.publishamerica.com
Baltimore

Printed in the United States of America

*To Janey, my lifelong friend, for her undying patience
during countless edits and her incredible way with words.
Most of all, her blind faith, encouragement and enthusiasm
makes anything possible.*

*This one's for you, with love
PK
June 2005*

Acknowledgments

I am grateful to so many that it is impossible to name them all here. They know who they are; thanks for your help and patience. A few must be mentioned, though: Patti McAlpine; Adam and Dr. Amy Bishop for pushing me along and helping with the Texas bits; Marg Crowell whose eagle eye was all-seeing.

Last but definitely not least is my latest treasure, without whom I would have made some inexcusable errors. Only 13, Courtney Kenley is a truly dedicated junior editor, keeping my perspective in line.

Prologue

Screams echoed through the crumbling tenement. Scurrying rats paused in their scavenging among rotten fish and putrid pieces of KFC, peered through the reeking darkness with beady pink eyes, and then went on about their business. Just a routine assault in the cold dampness of the abandoned New York slum. Slurred curses and wild laughter rattled through the rafters. The four Marauders, jail-bait bullies, had hauled in another victim.

A weak shaft of moonlight fought through cobwebs heavy with grime. Leaning against a splintered doorway, hands in pockets, dark head bowed, a tall, strong young man sobbed quietly. His shabby black jacket had a faded Marauders crest on the back.

"Tony! Oh thank God!" Cass screamed more in fear than pain now. "Help me! Hurry!" Relief surged through her, giving her strength and determination. Wrenching an arm free from her sweaty, cursing captors, she reached out to the only person in her miserable life that she trusted. Her friend. Her protector ever since she could remember. Clenching her teeth to keep from heaving the bitter bile from her tortured stomach, and with blood streaming down her bare arm onto the filthy floor, she shrieked once more, her throat raw.

"To-o-n-y!"

Sharp-clawed creatures shredded her throat; white-hot pain seared each scrape and knife wound on her body. Feeling herself sinking into a black hole, she thought she'd have to give up, to seek merciful oblivion. "No! Leave me alone—stop! Tony, hurry!" The fist that landed on her stomach caused the roiling bile to spew over her attackers. It also weakened Cass to the point where she felt she would surely have to give up.

No, Cass, no...never, ever quit. Don't sink to their rotten level. B-but I just can't...never hurt so bad in my life...maybe I'm dying...I hope so...

Strong and wiry in spite of just turning fifteen, Cass was drained of strength. She'd been battling these bullies for what seemed like hours. Fear drove her now. Smelling the foul stink of those creeps, plus the rotting garbage strewn across the sagging floor, made her want to puke again. With heart hammering in her ears, she made one final plunge to free herself. She understood now that there would be no help from Tony. He was a Marauder now; the jacket made him one of them. He'd finally given in to their threats and joined them. Heartbroken and desperate, rage rose like a fireball and she shrieked in triumph as she felt her nails rip through skin and plunge into an eye socket.

Agonized screams echoed through the derelict building. "Now you've done it, bitch." Rough hands grabbed her blue plaid shirt, tore it into shreds as they shoved her toward a door at the back. Blazing pain tore through her ribs and back. She had fought like a rabid wildcat, leaving raw and bloody furrows of torn flesh on more than one guy. Furious, they stepped up the force of their attack. More knives appeared.

"To-o-o-n-n-y..." Her final desperate plea went unheard, drowned out by terrified yelling, screaming and cries for help as two girls were shoved into the filth. Cass felt herself slip free as her tormentors rushed to help their buddies subdue the new captives. Without a backward glance, Tony raced to help them. A searing pain ripped across her chest as she watched her Tony grab a little blonde girl and hold her against the wall. Cass struggled to breathe. A trembling chill prickled her skin. She fought against passing out, fixing her battered eyes on Tony's Marauder jacket. He was just like all the rest: a tough guy, spreading fear and hatred wherever he went. Stark fury surged through her body.

I'll kill him! I trusted him! Face burning, teeth clenched, Cass gathered herself to leap on his back as groans and thumps and screams tore through the air. *No! I won't let him trash me like a piece of meat. He's just a jerk, a bully. I don't need him – I don't need anyone!*

Crushing disappointment settled like stone in her pounding chest; she could taste her hatred. Cass almost shouted out in defiance, remembering just in time that she was in no position to do something dumb. She had to move. Now. Angrily fighting back burning tears, she shrank into the shadows.

Now, raw animal instinct took over. In the stinking darkness, trembling with pain and fear, Cass crawled along the base of a wall until she came to a corner. Which way to turn? Shivering and desperate to put space between her and her attackers, she scrambled unsteadily to her feet and quickly felt her way along a slimy wall until a blast of air smelling of rotten eggs and old cabbage hit her.

That's outdoors! Go! Go! A partially open rusty door led to a rickety fire escape. Stunned by Tony's rejection and dazed by the beating she had taken, Cass felt no fear now, no pain, but silent gut-wrenching sobs wracked her body. Lying on her belly, she eased herself down, step by step, gripping sharp, rotten iron with bleeding fingers. Her legs stretched down full length in her desperate search for a foothold. With darkness swirling around her, she couldn't see how far up or down she was until one foot sank ankle deep into squishy muck.

Now that she felt free, fear and grating pain pressed into her consciousness. She fought against it. She couldn't go on much longer. Dread of what they'd do to her kept her dragging on through the slush. Where should she go? Who could she go to? No one. No one cared anymore. Not even Tony.

Please, somebody help me. I've got to get away. I can't see! I've got to keep moving. What if they find me...oh, please God, please...

Heart pounding, and weakened by the agony of her ordeal, she stumbled blindly into the night.

CHAPTER ONE

A soft whinny burrowed into her subconscious. A *horse*? Cass bolted upright, choked, fought for air, unable to save herself. Her wrists, ankles, were tightly knotted. The rope wouldn't give.

Eyes wide with terror and heart tearing at her chest, she scrambled for a foothold, clawed at her restraints. All in vain. Screaming and grabbing at unseen attackers, at black leather jackets. Gradually her eyes focused in the dim light. Covering her face with the sodden, down-filled pillow, sobs from her deepest reaches burst out, releasing the writhing anxiety within. Forcing herself to take deep breaths, her thundering heartbeat began to settle. Peeking around her pillow she knew she was safe in her own bedroom, overlooking the paddock. Willing herself to swallow the panic, she pushed her wet, snarled blonde hair off her face, and peeled off sweat-soaked floral sheets. A beautiful dawn broke through the airy bedroom window, bathing her in glorious warmth. Above the queen-sized bed hung a painting of the seashore; wet sand, glistening pastel-colored stones, lazy pools of water left behind by the outgoing tide; all bathed in the sun's rising glow. Framed in driftwood, the painting stretched the entire width of her bed, reaching up a good three feet. The pastel tones echoed around the room's decor, even down to the fluffy mats scattered over the blue-gray terrazzo floor. Such visual peace Cass had never known, and now it embraced her soul with warmth and comfort. Soft tears of relief traced a leisurely path down her ravaged face to add to the dampness of her pillow.

In the distance, rolling plains seemed to go on forever, interrupted only by borders of high, white plank fencing, mesquite and clusters of live oak. Sun glinted off the shiny coats of mares and foals as they grazed or frolicked in the lush pasture. Throwing her head back against the coral velvet padded headboard, she drank in the soothing scent of newly mown grass, jasmine and Mrs. Kiley's prized rose bushes, all borne on the gentle breeze that rustled through the live oaks. A mockingbird announced its contentment somewhere in the distance.

A click shattered the dreamy silence. Her door opened.

"Cass—what's the matter?" A mop of long, auburn hair peered around the bedroom door. Briana Kiley, almost sixteen, only daughter of Margaret and Patrick, stared bleary-eyed at the mess of the bed and its occupant. "You were screaming and..."

"Yeah, Cass, you woke me up." The tousled bed-head of riotous copper-red curls shoved past Bri and across to the bed.

"Sean—get back here. Get out." Bri's sharp voice sliced through Cass's fuzzy mind.

Still confused, one thing she knew for sure: she really was in her very own room at the Rocking K Ranch in the great state of Texas. That helped put things in focus. Loco and Bimbo, the calico housecats, strolled through the door, inspected Cass's fluffy white slippers by the bed and jumped onto the rumpled sheets. Loco leaped gracefully onto Cass's tummy, causing Cass to grunt in protest.

"Cass?" Bri hesitantly moved farther into the room, grabbed her ten-year-old brother by his arm and propelled him toward the door.

"Cass wants me here. Don't you, Cass? You had a nightmare, didn't you?" Sean spun out of Bri's clutches and leaned across the bed to pat Loco.

"I'm sorry, Bri. You're right, Sean. I had a bad dream." Her long fingers traced the livid scars on her thin forearm, tanned by the strong southern sun. Embarrassed, she wiped her tears with a corner of the sodden sheet, and then gently petted Loco who was now rubbing against her bare leg. "I'm okay. I'll go wash up now." Loco had other ideas. He pressed closer, encouraging Cass to run her hand over his soft, colorful fur. He smelled so good—he'd been in the hay barn.

"Well, uh, you sure you're okay? Do you want me to get Mom?"

"I'll get her," and Sean tore for the door.

"No! Please, no." Mortified that Mrs. Kiley would see her like this, she gently pushed the protesting cat off her lap and slid out of bed, heading for her luxurious all-white bathroom.

"I'll hurry. Thanks, Bri. See ya, Sean." She closed the door firmly and leaned against it. Emotions whirled and battled within her; horror from her memories of such a short while ago; joy because these people cared about her; grim determination never to fall prey to trust or to love ever again; a soft swirl of contentment that she didn't know what to do with. She wasn't really sure what the feeling was, but it made her feel so good.

I will be strong. This will not happen again. I will take whatever comes from here on, and I'll learn to be a Texan, too, even if it kills me. It's just for the summer. Her heart dropped to her boots. Just for the summer—then what? *I wonder if Mom's okay. Where did that come from?* As mothers go, Cass's mom, Glenda, didn't quite qualify. Rarely at their squalid rooms, on welfare, drugs and booze, meant Cass pretty well brought herself up. Tony lived down the hall and became her protector at a very young age. Glenda rarely cleaned the place, let alone their clothes. Yet Cass cared about her. Deep down, a definite bond stretched from her soul to her mother's, which every once in a while caused her to wonder about her, but never strong enough to even think about going back to New York. Ever.

Feeling refreshed after a quick shower, she pulled on soft new bleached Levi's, sunshine yellow t-shirt and white socks — the kind with the cushiony soles. Toes wiggled in pleasure. Dark brown and tan hand-stitched cowboy boots waited down in the huge mudroom near the back door with everyone else's gear. Her insides clutched at the thought of all the things she wanted to learn, all the things she'd already experienced.

"Cass? Are you up?" Mrs. Kiley's kind but firm voice echoed up the winding staircase and along the elegant oak off-white stucco hall.

"Yes, ma'am. I'll be right down." *Good. Briana didn't tell her mother what happened.* Checking in the oval mirror, Cass ran the brush through her ash-blonde hair that reached halfway down her back, one last time before clasping it at the back of her neck with a long leather bootlace. Grasping the ends of her shiny hair, she pulled them around and buried her nose in the silky strands. What a glorious smell — sort of like the wildflowers over near the woods. And it gleamed with so many shades of blonde that she never knew she had. Her mind flicked unbidden back to the cake of soap that lay beside the dirty, greasy kitchen sink, full of dishes and pots that had leftovers cemented to them. She'd never seen soap suds until she was in the hospital. *Best try to forget; best just to look ahead. Better get downstairs.*

With thumping heart and clenched teeth, she reluctantly turned from the mirror, mentally preparing herself to join the family grouped around the huge oak table. She always felt like a nobody. Well, she was, wasn't she? Even the once-vigilant

Tony Bellini turned his back on her. At this thought her brows drew together in a scowl and she scolded herself with a vengeance. *Stop thinking like that. Stop putting yourself down. No matter what it takes, I'll never be a nobody again. Ever.*

CHAPTER TWO

Still troubled, she curled up on the window seat and gazed at the vast expanse of rolling hills, blue sky and marshmallow clouds. Gathering Loco close, he snuggled and purred with a contentment that helped settle her jangled nerves. Not a skyscraper, parking lot, filthy street or ghetto in sight. At that moment she almost gagged on the remembered stink of the place that she once called home.

"I'll never set foot in New York City again," she solemnly vowed.

The hired hands (cowboys, she called them) made her uncomfortable, as did Matt. She hoped time would ease her distress. Would time make her a better person? Was she so horrible that even Tony stood back while she was being attacked?

If there's something wrong with me, I have to know what it is. I'll fix it. Maybe Mom knows. Gotta find her. I hate feeling this way. I'm a good person. I'll prove it.

"Cassandra!"

Cass jumped up, her heart thumping in her chest. Loco landed on the floor, tail whipping with indignation. *Oh crap, I've screwed up again.*

"Coming, Mrs. Kiley."

Dragging her feet, Cass joined the family seated at the breakfast nook. *Nook* made it sound small but it was a huge, tiled area divided from the super-modern kitchen by a long bar that sat five on carved pine stools. The Kileys, all talking at once across the cartwheel table, stopped their chatter.

After all these months Cass was struck dumb. Not one sound could she utter, so she studied the lush landscaping that encircled the gigantic diving pool and deck. The tall French doors fascinated her—all that sparkling glass that never seemed to get dirty. Bacon, toast and coffee smells were so good they made her stomach growl. Heaving a sigh, Cass turned.

"Hey, Cass."

"Mornin', Cass."

"Sit here beside me." Bri pulled out a chair. Cass envied Bri her gleaming auburn hair, like her dad's; so was her ability to make everything appear natural. Like now; she accepted it as a normal event to have a perfect stranger move into her home for months on end.

"No fair. She always sits by you." Looking a little more together than he did earlier, Cass felt a tug around her heart when she gazed into Sean's deep, green eyes, winked at him and sat in the chair Bri offered.

Cass felt awkward but fought the feeling. Tall, dark and handsome, Mr. Kiley grinned at her while Mrs. Kiley handed her a plate of eggs and bacon, nodded encouragement, and then continued to eat her own breakfast. Matt just stared at her. A replica of his father in many ways, Cass sensed a huge chip on his shoulder. She gave him a wide berth. Lessons learned from the misfits in the ghetto were hard ones, and rarely forgotten.

Meeting Matt's indigo blue eyes, hers bored into his, unblinking, while she parked her elbows on the table, picked up a strip of crisp bacon in her fingers, and stuffed it into her mouth.

17

Matt snickered.

"Matthew!" rumbled his dad.

Her shin received a sharp kick. When she looked at him, Sean shook his head a tiny bit and pointed to his bacon. *Oh! Forgot!* She fought to keep the next piece on her fork.

"What would you like to do today, Cass?" Mr. Kiley's question surprised her.

Why ask me? I know darn well you have chores to do. Tell me what we're doing, don't ask me!

Matt's earlier smirk managed to turn her golden morning into black mush. Fortunately, her thoughts remained inside her head.

Her response to Mr. Kiley was an indifferent shrug.

Mr. Kiley glanced at his wife. Their eyes met, and she announced she was going to call Sal about plans for her week's visit with her family, who lived just down the way. Did anyone want to speak to her? Cass's heart took a shocked leap. Feeling a moment of panic, her thoughts flew in every direction. Tears stung her eyes but didn't fall. Bacon lay forgotten beside the clotted egg yolk, and her fork froze in mid-air. A terrible urge to bolt through the French doors, run fast and far and never come back, overcame her. She shot to her feet; her fork clattered onto the tile floor.

Oh, please, please don't send me back! I'll work harder, I promise. You're begging, Cass. It won't work. I try to be like them, but I'm still just me. Half chewed toast and jam turned to sawdust in her mouth.

"You're sending me back," she blurted out, tears finally springing from the wells of her deep, green eyes as she headed for the door, her chair crashing to the floor.

Alarmed, and sitting closest, Mr. Kiley was on his feet and holding her tightly against his chest while exclaiming in a tortured voice, "Oh, Cass, no! Never!"

"Honey, what gave you that idea? You're our precious girl!" Mrs. Kiley joined her husband, swept the thick blonde hair behind Cass's ears and kissed her tenderly on the forehead.

"Cassy girl, sit. Come on. Sit right here by me." Mr. Kiley drew her empty chair snug up against his and gently allowed her to sit, but still kept his arm around her. Mrs. Kiley gave Bri the eye. Bri quickly stood and placed her chair close to Cass's other side for her mother. She herself stood, a warm hand on each shoulder as if to help drain whatever poison was at work in this special, sweet girl's mind.

"Talk, Cass," ordered Mr. Kiley, softly.

A chair smacked sharply against the table as Matt left the table in disgust.

"Matthew! You haven't been excused!" Mrs. Kiley's roar was scary.

"May-I-be-excused," slurred through angry lips, and he was gone.

"Let him go, Meg. I'll deal with him later. He needs a boot in the..."

"It's a rough stage he's reached, Pat. Have some faith in him." Turning to the now quietly sobbing Cass, she continued, "And our special girl here can't seem to get out of *her* rough stage, either. What is it, Cass? What brought this on?" Mrs. Kiley took Cass's chin in her hand and gently turned her head so she could peer into the troubled eyes. Sad, frightened eyes. It was at this point that Meg fully grasped the inner hell that this young girl had been trying to sort out alone, while seeming to others to be doing okay. She had been showing them only the part of Cass that Cass wanted them to see.

Wiping her eyes with a shaking hand and with head still bowed, Cass admitted it was the mention of Big Sal that had set her off.

"Bad memories, right?" Mr. Kiley refilled his cup with tepid coffee. "Kayla, is there any hot coffee left?" His booming voice could be heard for miles, so in the kitchen, their loyal maid had no difficulty.

"Fresh pot just finished dripping." Kayla answered as she appeared with the steaming coffee and retrieved the empty carafe.

Cass was only half aware of all this activity as she thought about how to answer Mr. Kiley. She was drained, emotionally and physically. Her head was jammed full of questions, doubts and fears. However, there also glimmered an unquenchable spark of hope, always threatened by negative thoughts and reactions which were second nature to this girl from the Big Apple. When she did speak, her voice was so soft as to be almost a breath.

"Yes, memories, I guess. I really, really like Big Sal. I don't think I could have survived without her. When I used to hear about shelters for kids, I thought it was sort of like *jail*. I was scared when they moved me from the hospital to Haven House. The head of it was Big Sal, and it wasn't a jail at all! Some bad kids were punished a bit, and they talked real dirty all the time, but only some of them.

"You know, Big Sal was the one that brought me posters of horses, and, like, magazines and stuff. It made me feel sort of weird, though, and the other kids said mean things to me because of it. I didn't care. I didn't need them. I didn't even talk or *think* like them, you know? Sal made me want to get better and visit places where there were horses. But…I…um…I just *can't* go back." She stared at her hands while talking. "And if I have to leave here, I will go where there are green fields with horses and cattle and dogs and open sky."

Suddenly lifting her head, her eyes bored into Mr. Kiley's as she announced, "I will run away. I promise. But I can take care of myself." Her chin lifted as if daring him to doubt one word of what she said. "Memories? I guess they'll follow me until I filter out the worst ones. The very best ones I will hold in my heart forever. You."

Silence.

After all, what could be said to a young girl who had every intention of looking ahead, of remembering the positives, and who already had a plan for the future?

"What about you guys helping me check the mares and foals? I want to have a look at the irrigation out there anyway." Mr. Kiley reached for the coffee pot.

Pot number three and everyone wandered back to the table, talking, planning the day. A family; the good, the bad and the ugly got sorted out around the old wagon wheel.

So another Saturday began. No school. When Cass arrived at the ranch in early January, she could hardly walk properly, so hadn't been to school at all.

"I'm going to work Willie on the line this morning," Matt declared. "I want him ready for Ft. Worth."

"Relax. You've plenty of time. Besides, that colt'll get so sick of being schooled on that fancy length of leather and chain, going in circles, backing up, standing stock still — well — hell, he's going to lie down and play dead one of these days." Through the laughter Mr. Kiley continued, "We'll all ride out together. I may need your help. And it'll be a way to get Cass into the routine of running a ranch. Her days of goofing off by riding in circles in the ring are over." Chuckles again — even Cass managed a weak grin. Matt left the table.

Ohmygod! I want this more than anything — but what if I screw up? I won't. I won't let myself. I'm getting good — Earl says I'm a natural. He wouldn't lie.

"Great idea," agreed Mrs. Kiley, her eyes sparkling with delight. "I haven't been out there in weeks. Kayla can take care of things here."

As if on cue, Kayla entered the kitchen. The vivacious Hispanic mother of four had been part of the Kiley household since before Sean was born. Her home was a brick single-story dwelling in what was called the Compound, a unique area where landscaped homes offered privacy, but were still close to the pool, playgrounds and barbecue pit. The ranch hands and their families enjoyed these comforts. Kayla's husband, Joshua, was the Rocking K's top trainer — tall, bow-legged with the reputation of "do it, do it now and do it right — or else!" Yet, with the horses, his gentle and patient nature worked miracles.

Never knowing what having a kind man around was like, Cass grew up steering clear of all males—and most females. Men caused pain of one kind or another in her little world. Fear welled within her when approached by any one of them. This was a reaction she vowed to conquer. She liked Earl, the real old wrinkled-up guy with the bushy white mustache. And Mr. Kiley was always so nice to her. Maybe he was okay, too.

Passing the office on her way to the mud room, she overheard the Kileys talking. Hearing her name, she stopped, felt guilty but strained her ears anyway.

"Pat, we're not doing enough; or maybe not the right things. I'm at a loss. Such a sweet girl to be so sad." Cass heard Mrs. Kiley sink into one of the cream leather overstuffed chairs by the desk.

"I agree, but what more can we do? She won't talk. I don't know if she even *likes* to ride or do any of the other stuff. I mean, she won't even come into Denton with us. But I *have* to let her experience new things now that she's strong enough. Maybe I'll stumble over something that'll give her a little fun. She even disappears when the kids are in school, for God's sake. Mind you, she's with Earl who's got her riding like she was born in the saddle, but I still feel we're letting her down, somehow. Meg, I love that little girl. She's just a kid. A badly hurt kid in so many ways. I don't intend to give up on her." Cass jumped as he slammed his huge open hands onto the polished oak desk.

"I'm going to ask Sal's advice. Tonight." Standing, Meg headed for the door. Cass scampered quietly into the mud room, grabbed her boots and sat on the padded bench. She felt sick. Stomach clenched in knots, heart hammering, and tasting the sour tang of fear.

Sal! Big Sal! Are they going to send me back already? No freaking way! Dallas – that's where I'll go. I can get there and they'll never find me. But I don't want to go. What did I do? Maybe Matt said something. But I've hardly had anything to do with Matt. This not knowing is making me crazy.

A tear escaped as she pulled on her new hand-stitched boots and headed out the door before Mrs. Kiley saw her. The kids swore that she could read minds. Jesse and Sam, the Australian Blue Heeler dogs, raced up to greet her. Scrambling for attention was Stray. Caked with dirt and skinny as a rail, she had wandered onto the ranch about a year ago and decided she liked the Rocking K. They called her "the stray" for a long time, but it eventually became just Stray. They figured she was mostly Border collie, but whatever, she had clung to Cass like glue since her arrival. They all figured she knew a kindred spirit when one crossed her path.

She knows I don't have a home either. Maybe she can come to Dallas with me and then nobody would dare hurt me. Bending down Cass gently rubbed Stray's soft, black ears. Stray grinned. Cass giggled.

Stressed out by the proposed phone call to Sal, on top of the bad feeling that Matt left her with at breakfast, Cass wrote to her mother that evening. Addressing the envelope to the grocer at the corner of their street in New York, she knew he'd find her mom if she was still around.

Mom – where are you? Are you all right? I haven't seen you since before Christmas, you know, that week of the storm? After that I got beat up by the Marauders and Tony let them. The police took me to the hospital then I went to a place called Haven House. A woman called Big Sal sent me here to live with her uncle's family on a ranch. I'm fine now. Mom, I'm always scared. I want to stay here but I think they know I'll turn out like you and are going to send me back.

This is important, Mom. I saw on TV that addicts have babies who aren't healthy. That they might grow up as addicts, too. Were you high all the time back then? You always told me not to try any pills or booze or stuff, and I haven't. If you knew all this, why are you still using them? Is it a sickness? Have I got it? If I do, tell Big Sal so I can maybe change. I want them to like me. I'm not coming back to New York no matter what. I hope you get this letter. I hope you're okay. I wish you were happy.

Cassy

CHAPTER THREE

"Pssst!"

Cass stopped, turned. Nothing. Leaving the mud room, she headed for the kitchen, admiring the awards, photos and trophies that lined the white stucco hall. Whiffs of lemon from highly polished woodwork made her feel good. Antique carriage lamps served as lighting, and the wood trim was thick, dark oak. The same burgundy tile as the entry and mud room continued throughout the downstairs.

"Pssst! Cass!" This time she spotted the red curly head peering out of Mr. Kiley's office doorway.

"Sean! What are you doing in there?" They were whispering even though no one was home.

"Come here. Look what just came in on the fax." Sean scampered across the room, grabbed the papers and shoved them at her.

"No. You're not supposed to look at private papers, and you know it."

"But it's all about *you!*"

That still doesn't make it right. But what if it's about sending me back to New York? Everyone's out now. I could run away before they get home.

"This is wrong, Sean." She took the papers. He peered eagerly over her arm, blocking the page. "Scram! I can't read!"

The first three pages were about the sale of horses. The fourth was about a meeting at the kids' private school. Then, there it was. Headed "Fax Cover Sheet, HAVEN HOUSE, NY," addressed to Pat Kiley, from Sally Ross, Administrator.

I don't want to read this. What if — but I've got to know what's going to happen to me. What'll I do if — ? Darn. Stomach cramps. Fear.

"Hurry up, will you?"

"Here! We'll read it together," and she placed the sheet on the corner of the antique desk.

It began:

Hey, Uncle Pat!

Hope all's well. Below I've listed what I believe you want to know, and should know, about Cassandra LeDrew. Also some advice. Any questions, call.

LeDrew not her real name — no relatives found

Found beaten, badly injured, unconscious in filthy, slush-filled gutter

Wouldn't or couldn't identify attackers, but said there were at least four

Escaped when two other girls were being beaten

Unbelievable ordeal, but she recovered physically; still carries visible scars

Incredible courage. Needs time to deal with her inner demons…

"Why'd she have to blab all this stuff? Why can't I just be me?" Cass felt betrayed. She didn't think Big Sal would tell everybody everything. She trusted her.

"Well how are we supposed to know what you like to do if nobody tells us? Do you want us to play twenty questions every day? What's that word mean?" and he pointed to "Incredible."

"Nothing. Let me finish before someone comes."

...Advice: The great outdoors will be her salvation initially, and then will come the "whole family" image. Loves horses but has never been near one, so that will be the obvious "hook"...

Hook! Hook for what? For horses? What's going on?

...She trusts no one; she believes in nothing. Her life has been one of survival of the fittest, but she did get her schooling – it was the only sane thing in her world and she did well. I suggest you treat her as one of your own. Daily chores must be done, done right and done on time. Give her a horse of her very own to be completely responsible for. Teach her to ride as if her life depended on it – professional level...

Cool! My own horse! I can do all this stuff – I'll show them I'm no slum rat!

...No pussy-footing around, Uncle Pat. Be up front with her, be honest even if the truth hurts, praise her for her accomplishments. All these things will lead to trust. She needs to learn to trust. She needs to knock down that brick wall she's built around herself...

Brick wall, right! More like a thick skin – it's safer. Bricks can be knocked down, but no one's going to mess with my head. Let them try!

...I believe that quality time spent with you and your kids will be the best experience of her life. She's only 15 but has lived a very tough life. Your way of living will be strange to her, so be patient. Answer

all her questions and show her all about the ranch. Be open; be yourselves. I love that girl, Uncle Pat, so take good care of her for me.
See you in a few weeks.
Love to all,
Sally

She loves me? Really? Is that what I felt for her? Then why am I scared to go back?

Cass just stood there, stared at the page, turned it over then stared at it again. Fear was trying to worm itself into her belly, yet her teeth were clenched in determination. Thoughts, memories good and bad were swirling around in her head. *What does all this mean? Do I get to stay a little longer? I must – she said to give me chores and teach me to ride.*

"Crikey, put it back. Someone's coming," and Sean bolted for the door, stopped short and ran back to the fax machine. "No, Stupid, turn them *this* way or they'll know someone's been reading them." He quickly rearranged the faxes and the two of them made for the door, stopped, peeked down the hall, then with hands in pockets and an innocent swagger they headed for the mud room.

Sneaky little twerp – he's done this before!

"Let's go see which horse you like, then it won't take so long when Dad asks you."

"Well, we can look, I suppose, but we can't let on we know he's going to give me one, can we." Cass slid him a look that said it all, shoved open the door, wondering if he was going to get them in trouble. A nonstop blabbermouth, a lot of what he'd told her so far was stuff about their life on the ranch and about their relatives – some of whom he didn't like. She'd just have to trust him. *Trust. Yeah. Got to start somewhere.*

"Halloo! Anybody home?" Mrs. Kiley was home with the groceries. That meant all hands should go help unload the silver Grand Cherokee.

A door opened and shut. That would be Kayla. Sean and Cass stopped and looked at each other.

"We'd better help," and Sean turned back. "Come on!"

"I'm going for a walk," Cass declared, and ducked into the glorious, aroma-filled rose garden. Jesse and Stray must have been laying in wait for her, and streaked from behind a huge, bloom-laden trellis to join her. Greeting them both, she strode down the path and disappeared among the thick pines, her furry companions frolicking around her.

"Walk! Where you going to walk to?" yelled Sean, watching as Cass melted into the shadows of the pines.

Silence except for the rustle of leaves, the amazing songs of the mockingbirds as they cleverly imitated so many other birds, and the panting of her two faithful companions. Her thoughts raced unchecked, upsetting her, but soon she focused on what was gnawing at her subconscious. Fear. But she hadn't felt fear during all those years in New York. She was too busy outwitting her tormentors. So why feel afraid now? Because she would have to leave this place that she now thought of as home? Fear of being flung back onto the streets of the ghetto? Sal's letter said that she loved her. Well, she sure kept close to her after the attack. Every day she appeared at the hospital — then moved her to Haven House. And as each day passed, Cass watched that door like a hawk, putting up with the discomfort of dressing changes, stitches being removed and limbs being painfully exercised. Always watching. At the first sight of Sal, or sound of her voice, Cass's insides became calm, her breathing settled and her lips relaxed into a shy smile of anticipation.

At Haven House she had no choice but to endure the bullying of a few, the silent stares of most, and the anxiety of wondering what would happen next. But then Sal would appear, each and every day, and they'd sit in a corner to chat about the day's events. Somehow, though, Sal would sense when Cass was really troubled. On those days she'd take her to her office, close the door, and really get down to the root of things. One day she appeared with a huge poster of a black horse and tacked it to Cass's wall. This was followed by issues of Western Horseman, which Cass ate up. Cass felt changes within herself; a warmth, and the comfort of sharing her private thoughts, good and bad. Trust. Maybe that was it. If that was for real then why fear being sent back? She'd have Sal. But not for long. She'd be sixteen in a few months, and she'd have to leave Haven House anyway.

Suddenly the thought of seeing Sal again stirred her to mild excitement. Cass could ask her all the questions that she wouldn't dare ask Mr. or Mrs. Kiley. Sal knew her — *really* knew her, and she could say and ask whatever she wanted without being afraid of putting her foot in her mouth. Now she was more determined than ever to improve her horsemanship — they said she was a natural and doing just great — but she wanted Sal to be surprised, to be proud of her.

Sighing deeply, feeling much better, Cass called to the dogs and strode off, aiming for home. *I can handle this — no problem. Stop being such a wimp. Just be yourself — that's what Sal always told her.*

CHAPTER FOUR

Head down, thoughts awhirl, Cass wandered back through the pine grove. Needing to be alone, she slipped in behind the compound and through the trees to the mares' pasture. The dogs, sensing her confusion, quietly nosed around the trees, never straying more than a few yards from her.

So quiet. She stopped, looked around as if for the first time, but this time the peace was truly visible, worming its way into her soul. It still didn't seem real to her. All the comforts she quickly learned to accept in the huge, sprawling ranch house—her very own, very special bedroom with private bath; yummy food and lots of it; a clothes closet that was rapidly filling up with her very own things—were exciting, sure enough, but also overwhelming. Who wouldn't wade into such luxury and not be affected by it? But it wasn't real to Cass. She was just passing through and would be gone in a few months. She couldn't allow it to penetrate her defenses. Not knowing what was in store for her was a truth that kept letting the air out of her balloon. Emotions were not permitted to soar with hope, pleasure or confidence. Maybe now, though. Maybe now she could safely allow a bit of acceptance to trickle in. What harm could it do? She had herself under tight control, didn't she?

She approached a group of mares and their foals. Most of the foals were stretched out in the relative coolness of the shadows cast by lofty live oaks and pine. Smiling to herself, she remembered asking how come they were called *live* oaks, when they were obviously alive and growing. Just another species of evergreen tree. Weird name. The mares stood head down, still as statues until an irksome fly caused a tail to switch or an ear to turn. Cass and the dogs stood motionless, not wanting to disturb this scene of pure bliss. In this way it would be imprinted on her mind for future visits to her memory bank. No matter where she ended up or what happened to her, Cass knew she could draw on these memories to help her through whatever life had in store for her.

The fax from Big Sal disturbed her. No big deal, but as much as she owed Sal, she was uncomfortable that someone else was messing with her life, her independence. What independence? These seventy acres of Texas and all it held sure didn't spell independence. To Cass, being alone and calling all the shots in her life had been pure hell. But it was her life to live; her decision to sneak through back alleys to get to school without being threatened. So, she went days on end without anything to eat. She drank water. Instead of going out on the streets with the other kids, she stayed in the one-room hovel, reading anything she could lay her hands on. Tony would check on her whenever he came by, sometimes bringing her food and staying to talk with her about all kinds of stuff. He warned her about people and places to avoid at all costs. When she was sick, he'd check on her morning and night.

And when she was in danger, being attacked, beaten and torn, he walked away.

Cass snarled, spun around, and strode back to the pine grove, causing her bodyguards to sniff the wind for danger. They sensed her renewed anger and knew she felt pain. The abrupt movement caused the mares to throw up their heads and snort in alarm. Ears pricked forward and nostrils flared, testing what they saw and smelled, and deciding it was okay. She belonged here. All was well. They resumed their peaceful slumber.

So—horses were to be a hook. Horses were supposed to make her happy, make her feel like one of the family. Humph! It would take more than that, because *she* was her own person. *She* would decide what would make her happy. Happy. What was that?

Aware she was sliding into self-pity, and determined not to, Cass lifted her chin and threw her shoulders back. Okay. She was ready. Bring on the Kileys, even that big shit Matt Know-it-all who she purposely avoided. Bri was relaxed and comfortable to be around, so Cass knew there was no problem there. Sean was a little hellion, but seemed to be on Cass's side should a battle erupt. Cass laughed to herself. There would be no battles fought at the Rocking K—it was too perfect. Mr. and Mrs. Kiley were straight out of a TV family show. She liked them, she really did, but somehow they were out of reach, even though they were in the same room, talking to her, including her in everything. Or, just maybe, was she herself keeping *them* at a distance?

"Where've you been? All the work's done so you came back, right?" Sean. He kept showing up like a bad smell. "Know what? We just had a family con...con...meeting and it was all about you and that fax." He looked up at her, full of importance.

Cass's heart plunged. Dread seeped into the space where it had been.

Go away, Sean! Go away, Kileys! I can't be what you want me to be because it's not the way life really is. I want to leave. Now. I don't belong here. I don't fit in.

Heaving a deep sigh, she admitted to herself that she was afraid.

"Matt doesn't want to be bothered with you," continued the shrill voice. "He says to just let you be a guest, ride a quiet horse, feed you three times a day and then say bye-bye. Simple. And then do you know what he said to *Dad*?" Sean was awed by the words he was about to repeat. He didn't wait for a response from Cass. "He asked Dad, y' know, in his real snotty voice, if he was already getting a branch ready for *you* on our precious Family Tree!" With green eyes wide and face flushed, Sean waited for a reaction.

He didn't get one.

Cass was scared to move or open her mouth in case she barfed.

Sean was not going to shut up. More was coming, she could tell.

"But Bri thinks it's cool to be getting a sister and says she'll take you under her wing. First she'll have to grow wings," and he erupted into gales of laughter at his own joke.

"What's so funny?" demanded Matt, rounding the corner of the house, spotting his little brother with *that girl* at the edge of the pine grove. "Where do you think you're going? Kayla's putting lunch on the table and sent me to find you guys. C'mon." His vivid blue eyes bored into Cass's. "You want a special invitation, Miss New York?" Sarcasm dripped off every word. "Those dogs were supposed to be working, by the way."

Cass watched him disappear back to the house and didn't know which was worse, not knowing why he hated her so much or having to go sit down to lunch knowing what she now knew. Taking a deep breath and slipping back as far as she could behind her brick wall, she slung her arm around Sean's neck and began to haul him up the path.

"Time to eat, ol' buddy," and Sean gazed up at her in wordless adoration.

Removing their boots in the mud room, they washed their hands in the set-tub at the end of the room, and then headed down the long hall toward the kitchen.

Matt appeared at the door of his father's office, carrying a big framed picture.

"Hey, Cass! Ever seen a Family Tree?" he challenged.

"I don't even know what one is," she admitted defiantly, head up, eyes burning into his. *Okay! Lay it on, fella! I've decided you don't count, tree or no tree. You're a jerk!*

"Here, let me show you," and he lay the heavy glass and oak framed document down on the hall table. Pointing to a branch on a leafless tree full of limbs with names on them, he gloated, "here I am. And here's Bri, and Sean. And Mom and Dad are up here. And then my grandparents, both sets; and great-grandparents, both sets; and great-great—"

"Shut up, Matt, and go to the kitchen," barked the big man himself.

Cass started down the hall, but he held her by the arm. "Cassandra, I don't know what's going on in that boy's head, but I ask you to please forgive him if he hurt you. He knows darn well you don't know what that tree is all about. He was digging at you. It's not you, dear; it's himself he's at war with."

Putting his arm around her shoulders, and tousling Sean's curly head, they headed to the kitchen.

In spite of Mr. Kiley's kind words, Cass felt like the worst kind of misfit. She realized fully what their Irish heritage meant to them, and her nose had been well and truly rubbed into her own bleak beginnings. She didn't even know who her *father* was for god sake, and they all knew it. A true, flesh and bone nobody straight from the gutters of the Big Apple. What's the point of all this crap? Whatever's going on here within this family, she didn't want any part of. With plenty of her own troubles, she sure didn't want to add to theirs. Each day she felt closer and closer to the Kileys, their hired hands, and especially Sean. But enough is enough. She didn't want to cause a rift in their family. She sadly remembered the high she felt earlier when remembering Sal. So fleeting. So fickle.

The next morning Cass slipped the letter to her mother into the big pocket of Kayla's starched white apron. Kayla looked up in surprise when the hand disappeared into her pocket.

"Kayla, please don't say anything to anybody, okay? Could you mail this for me? Soon? It's very important," Cass pleaded, her face crimson.

Kayla smiled, nodded, and late that evening passed the unopened letter on to Mr. Kilcy.

CHAPTER FIVE

"Where the hell did Matthew Collin Kiley go? You're only seventeen years old and already you're the biggest pain in the butt in Texas!" Pat Kiley's deep roar easily penetrated the heavy oak door to his office. "You're getting rough with the horses; you're bossy and crude with the hands; you treat your family as if we're all diseased—and now this shameful attitude toward Cass. I know the teen years can be..."

"Yeah, yeah, yeah. Here comes the same old, same old." Matt's chair scraped across the floor as he started for the door.

Cass was on her way to saddle up Old Yeller when the outburst from Matt's father stopped her in her tracks. She didn't intend to listen, but the accusations being flung at Matt were scary. Hearing him scrape his chair back, she hurried down the hall, hoping to be around the corner before the door opened.

"Get your sorry ass back here! Now! Don't you ever, *ever* speak to me like that again, you hear me, Matthew?" This time Cass was sure she saw the walls shake. Stopping, she leaned back toward the office. This was drama of the first order.

"So I'm a sorry ass, too, am I? Add it to the list, Dad, and head it 'My Son, the Failure', then pin it to the almighty Family Tree to make sure future generations are made aware of the black sheep amongst all the flawless saints you're always cramming down my throat!" Matt's retort increased in volume until, at the end, his voice cracked.

"Sit down," his father said in a more normal voice. "Matthew, there's a problem here. How would you like it handled?"

Cass sidled closer to the door.

"No, sir! You're not gonna suck me into saying what I really think just so you can throw it back in my face." He spat out the words.

"Listen to yourself, son. You're angry. Real angry. That's not healthy; get it out — let's hear it. Maybe there's an answer. You can't go on like this, Matt."

"Okay. Here's one answer." Sarcasm dripped as Matt foresaw his dad's reaction. "Let me show Willie on the line at Ft. Worth, then at the World Congress in Ohio. It's only fair. I'm the one who halter broke him, taught him how to stand to be groomed — all that stuff — and now I have him working on the line real good! That would prove you trust me."

"That's impossible. Willie is being readied and trained as a reining horse and eventually will be sold as a stud. He's a future gold mine and has to be handled in the ring by a top professional. And that's Joshua. You're barely seventeen. We've got plenty of young horses for you to train and show in Youth…"

"I'm almost eighteen!" Matt was shouting now. "You won't give me my own car; you won't let me show the colt I trained; I'm rough; I'm crude; I've got no sense of humor or compassion. Hell, Dad, I just don't meet the Kiley standards at all, do I? So fire me! Do us all a favor! You have a new toy to manipulate now so I won't be missed at all. If you showed me the care and concern you've shown that blonde bitch from the gutter these past few months I'd probably have turned out different. Cut my branch off the damn Family Tree and nail one on for Cassy-baby, only lose the LeDrew — definitely not Irish!"

A chair crashed followed by a resounding whack. Silence. Cass was shaking like a leaf. *Where should I go? What should I do? Enough. No more running away. Time to grow up and take control, Cass girl.* She wheeled around and smacked into Sean. He'd heard it all and gave her a shove all the way through the house and out onto the terrace.

"Crikey! Dad's lost it! He *never* whacks us. Never. Wait'll Mom hears about this."

Cass couldn't tell whether Sean was fearing or looking forward to a family feud.

"I'm not staying where I'm not wanted, Sean. I'm better now. I'm leaving. Your family has saved me in more ways than you know, but it's time to leave." Seating herself on a bright yellow cushioned patio chair, she placed her elbows on the sparkling glass tabletop.

"Listen up, Cass. You're not going anywhere. They won't let you. Besides you got it all wrong. We do so like you. You just got to learn some stuff." He paused, drew an imaginary figure on the table top then, in his youthful, tactless, open manner he ran his tanned fingers through his unruly mop of hair and blurted, "Go out before breakfast like everybody else and help with chores; stop staring at everybody and never saying anything; fight, laugh, cry, yell — that stuff; don't be such a slob at the table — that's gross; don't be so picky — eat what's on your plate — "

"Are you finished, Mister Know-It-All?" Cass was furious. Slamming her fists onto the table she tipped a glass over, soaking a pile of cocktail napkins. She shook, stammered trying to say more, but only an anguished "*Jeez!*" blurted out. He'd hurt her. The mouthy little twerp.

"No I'm not finished, and don't swear. You're too skinny. Eat. Be nicer to the guys — they try to help and you walk away and hurt their feelings. And you got to start talking. Now. Here's the plan. I've got it all figured out. You're a whole lot better than when you first got here — boy! What a mess! And you talked funny — bad words and stuff. But now I'll be your coach on how to act and stuff, but it will be our secret. Deal?"

Cass gaped at him, speechless.

"There, you're doing it again!" and for the first time in her life Cass broke into a full-blown belly laugh. Did it ever feel good. She wasn't sure what she felt, but somewhere deep inside her, something relaxed, opened up and was slowly filling with warmth.

"I don't know what I'd do without you, you little beast." Yanking a fistful of red hair, she added, "Now it's my turn. What is that stupid word you use all the time? Is it supposed to be a swear word?"

"What — Crikey? I don't know. Think I read it somewhere or saw it on TV. What's the matter with it? I like it. It's me. Now let go my hair!"

Their laughter echoed into the family room where Mrs. Kiley was replacing glasses on the bar shelves.

"Hey, you two! Going to share the joke?" she called out to them, which only made them laugh harder.

CHAPTER SIX

"Cass, relax!" Bri shouted across the training paddock. Proudly perched on Old Yeller, a retired palomino brood mare, Cass sensed her joy in carrying awkward beginners round and round in circles. Well past that stage herself, having worked hard with Earl for over two months, she tried to fend off boredom. Every once in a while, with the real greenhorns, Yeller would stop dead, shake all over, stand with one hind foot resting on its toe, drop her head and close her eyes. Siesta time. Nothing would budge her until she was good and ready to carry on with her duties. Now when she pulled her stunt, everyone stood around chatting, went to the stable for a soda or to use the washroom. The instructor took the opportunity to explain the finer points of riding to the student, still in the saddle, so no one resented Old Yeller's siestas. She didn't take many, usually only one per greenhorn. However, there had been certain obnoxious people who decided they were going to learn all there was to know right this minute because it sure didn't look that hard to do. Word would quickly make the rounds that they had another "winner" in the ring, and all hands would saunter over to bear witness to the decline and fall of yet another of Yeller's victims. She seemed to know who the jerks were even though they were friends of friends of the Kiley's. The Rocking K wasn't a riding academy, but often someone in the family asked if so-and-so could get some pointers on reining, equitation, barrel racing and so on. Less often a "winner" would appear, usually someone visiting friends in the Denton/Aubrey area who knew the Kileys well. Little kids were great, responsive and got the basics quickly – at least enough so they could safely ride Old Yeller around in the paddock for as long as they liked, or until Old Yeller decided to call a halt for the day.

This morning, however, Cass was feeling totally at home perched atop the smooth old Quarter Horse. The first time she sat in the saddle she had found herself holding her breath, waiting for disaster to strike, every muscle taut and heart pounding double-time. Through many hours of patience from Earl, Pat Kiley, Bri and even Sean, Cass learned that her love for horses, which had grown through books and magazines, was real. She now felt an eagerness within her that was demanding more; new experiences; bigger challenges.

"I am relaxed," she retorted. "This is the way I feel most comfortable. Earl says it's okay." Cass walked the horse over to the rail where Bri was standing, looked over at Earl sitting on his bale of hay, silently watching her progress. He winked and nodded his head.

"Your ears are always in line with your heels now, and you sit the jog real smooth," piped up Sean, wiggling through the fence rails and offering Yeller a chunk off his apple.

"Thanks, Sean. So now you figure I'm ready for the Congress, right?" Cass teased, referring to the gathering of top Quarter Horses, riders, buyers and breeders to ever assemble at one show, held yearly in Columbus, Ohio, a World Class event.

"Well…maybe first you should try a bunch of horses to see if you can stay on them all." These words of wisdom, although extreme, bore a seed of truth.

"Yeah, you're right. You've been on Yeller too long, and it's time you really got to work on a working horse. Besides you must be bored to tears by now." Bri adjusted the throat strap under Yeller's soft, cream-colored neck.

"No way! We're friends," and she stroked Yeller's white mane, feeling the thick, wavy hair run through her fingers, always so clean in spite of her habit of rolling on the ground in absolute bliss after being ridden. "What horse do I get on next? Is it quiet?" Suddenly butterflies were let loose in her tummy. Was it fear or excitement? Cass decided it was excitement because she didn't want it to be fear. She had known enough fear to last a lifetime.

"Here comes Earl," Bri murmured. "Who's he got with him? Is he drunk or high? Matt's bringing up the rear. This should be interesting."

Cass dismounted, held the reins close to the bit, and walked over to the gate, studying the newcomer. No. He wasn't drunk. He was just a blow-hard cocky city shit, swaggering along beside Earl, toward Cass. The look on Earl's face was one of pure disgust.

"Hey! You Cass?" The city boy tilted his head to one side and looked her up and down.

Cass returned the favor, head to one side, and saw a handsome, blond six-footer with blue eyes half hidden by droopy eyelids (supposed to look sexy). The "look" failed because of pouting lips and a goatee, which must have had all of a dozen limp hairs in it. She looked him straight in the eye, lifted a saucy eyebrow, and led Yeller around him toward the stable. Proud that she could now handle herself around strangers, even men, she allowed herself a mental pat on the back.

"Hey, babe, I'm here to ride that horse, right, Matt?"

Stopping in her tracks, Cass again eyed this ignorant piece of crap with a withering stare, took two steps toward him and grated out through clenched teeth, "Don't you ever call me that again. *Ever!*" and whirling to face Matt, snapped, "That goes for you and the rest of your brain-dead friends!" Without another word, she shoved the reins at Matt and strode over to Earl, heart banging in frustration. Bri and Sean joined them. Before long the hands sauntered closer to the paddock. They hadn't had a "winner" in a long time. Maybe they were about to get lucky. This was Cass's first and, still grinding her teeth, she could hardly wait.

"You're doing fine, Missy, just fine," murmured Earl without looking at her. "But you need a different horse. Which one?"

"Um...well...Earl, I don't know which one I'll be allowed to ride. No one has said anything." She kept her eye on Matt's friend. If this was to be a blowout she didn't want to miss anything. Feeling a warm body press against her leg, Cass glanced down to find Stray grinning up at her, sensing excitement in the air. Squatting on her heels, she hugged the wiggling creature close, rubbing her ears. Pine scent wafted to her nostrils; she'd been down playing in the grove again.

"You're a natural, for sure. Got a long ways to go, but not on that there Yeller horse. After this young punk gets his brains bashed into his pants we'll go looking for your horse."

"We can't just go out..." Cass's protest was cut short by Bri's sharp elbow in her ribs. Cass turned, saw where Bri's eyes were aimed, the suppressed grin, and settled in to watch the action.

"That's Snake Meredith! Oh, Crikey! I heard Dad tell Matt those guys aren't allowed here anymore because of them leaving the mares' gate open last time. Oooweee! I hope Yeller gets him good."

"Sean, don't say that. What if he gets hurt?" Bri had to act like a big sister and try to steer him into gentler thoughts.

Matt held Yeller's bridle as Snake strode up and stuck the wrong foot in the stirrup on the wrong side of the horse. Before anything drastic could happen Matt snapped, "No, Snake. Don't get up on that side. You'll end up sitting backward—besides, she'll dump you." He grinned at his friend who was not the least put off by this obvious goof, and ignoring the grins of his audience, Snake swaggered around behind the horse. He didn't get kicked, thanks to the old mare's good manners. An awkward scramble got him onto the saddle, headed in the right direction. Taking a death grip on the reins, he dug his heels sharply into Yeller's sides, jerked her head around and aimed her through the paddock gate.

"Snake! No! Stop! Stay inside the fence! Stop jerkin' on her! Stop kickin' her! Jeez, man, are you nuts?" Matt was racing across the immense lawn, yelling and trying to head them off before they reached the formal flower gardens near the house. But horse and rider were covering a lot of ground, fast. Yeller swerved to avoid shrubs and trees, causing Snake to slide farther down the side of the saddle. He was hanging onto the saddle horn with one hand and her long, white mane with the other. Matt gave up trying to do anything and stood, hands on hips like the rest of them, waiting to see how this show was going to end.

The eager onlookers hardly had time to assemble near the wide expanse of velvety lawn before Yeller saw her chance. Still at the full gallop, beautifully groomed Bermuda grass tearing up in huge chunks from her pounding hooves, she veered to the left, ducked her head and stopped dead. Snake kept right on going, hit the ground screaming, rolled and bounced right into the fish pond. This was home to the large and expensive Japanese Koi fish which were Pat Kiley's pride and joy.

"Yay, Yeller! You got him!"

"Shut up, Sean. He could drown in there," but no one seemed to be in a hurry to rescue the stupid jerk.

When he finally got himself sorted out, Snake stood in water up to his butt with fancy pond grass hanging off him every which way. With a bloody nose, torn shirt and soaked to the skin, he tried to make a graceful exit out of the slippery, rock-framed pond, and failed miserably. When he finally slipped and stumbled onto solid ground he looked neither left nor right, but limped in filth-covered dignity out of sight toward the car park. His left Nike had vanished.

The hoots and laughs must have been heard in the next county as his audience slowly made their way back to the stable area.

Old Yeller was already in her stall munching contentedly on the rich hay from the hayrack in the corner of her stall. It didn't matter to her that she still had a bit in her mouth and a saddle attached to her. She nickered proudly as Cass and Bri approached her stall.

"Well done, old girl. That's one ass that won't be back." Bri broke into laughter again as she undid the girth. "Oh, Cass, I almost forgot. Earl wants to see you in the school barn."

"C'mon, Cassy, I'll go with you." Sean pulled her by the hand.

"Don't you want any help here?" Cass felt the need to walk alone with her thoughts. So much to think about; scary things; exciting things. Different horses; shows; new people. Biting down on her lower lip, she frowned. *Will I be good enough? I'm not afraid to try…I don't think.*

"Nope. I'll rub her down and check her for damage, then I'm off to the house. It's getting near supper time." Looking up, she asked, "Are you okay, Cass?"

"Yeah. Sure. I won't be long. See ya," and Cass jogged alongside Sean down the lane to the big open-sided stable near the compound. Earl sat waiting for her.

"That fella won't dare show his face around this town again," announced the old man, his black eyes sparkling, and deep crinkles spreading into his snow-white hair. He enjoyed the show. "Yep, it was funny, but could have been real bad. Never say you can do something you can't. No shame in saying you don't know — show me. Damn pride will get you in trouble every time."

Cass was enthralled with this old man. He never raised his voice ever, no matter what, and he always said things that Cass found herself thinking about long afterward.

"So. What kind of riding are you planning on doing?" The kind, black eyes squinted at her.

"Barrels," piped up the red-headed mouthpiece.

Cass gave him a dirty look before answering Earl. "It doesn't matter what kind. I'd just like to be a good rider, like Bri. Maybe if I get the chance I'd like to try different things."

"Good girl." He slid off the back of the manure spreader and headed for the pasture. "There's some I don't want you to mess with just yet, but you take a look around and see which one you'd like to try."

Together they entered through the side gate and approached a band of about ten horses, all dozing in the long shadows of the late afternoon sun. Sean wandered over to a much smaller black horse and hugged its neck. Banjo had been his horse since he started to ride, but was now retired. Cass had wandered through here many times and, although she didn't know them by name, she had become friends with several of them. Her eyes searched for her favorite as she ran her hand down the neck of an especially colorful Paint mare. Her coat shone like a burnished chestnut which set off her white markings to perfection. This included a patch on her side that Pat Kiley insisted was the map of Ireland. Cass knew *her* name, of course. Shamrock, and she was strictly off limits.

A soft upper lip mussed through her hair, startling her. "Oh! It's just you, you silly thing," and she scratched between the ears of a tall, glossy black gelding. "How ya doin', fella?" He answered by rubbing his head up and down her arm, almost pushing her off her feet. He smelled of warmth, fresh air and unmistakably horsy.

"That there's Pine Image. Top bloodlines but he doesn't move like he should. Sound as a dollar, willing to go anywhere, but there's something missing. Can't figure him out. Too bad. Good horse." Earl reached under his battered hat and scratched his head.

"But all the others seem shorter. How come he's so tall — and so black?"

"Born to a mare that was bought about four years ago. They never knew she was in foal for months, and didn't know who the papa was. This is what appeared, and the boss doesn't want to sell him for some reason. Well, come on, girl, it's getting late and I'm hungry. The old lady's making a mess of fajitas tonight. Which horse are you going to pick?"

"Earl, I can't walk out here, point to a horse and say it's mine — even just for the summer. Mr. Kiley should be the one to let me know if I can have a horse." Cass felt guilty just *thinking* about choosing a horse for herself.

"He told me to get you one. So get one and hurry up."

Sean came barreling up at that point.

"You never learn *anything*, do you?" Earl spun Sean around by the shoulder. "How many times do you got to be told *not to run around the horses*, eh, boy?" He clipped him sharply on top of the red curls and turned back to Cass.

"Aren't you going to help me? I don't know anything..." Stammering, she shrugged, feeling helpless and uncomfortable.

"That's right. You don't...so...which one *feels* right?"

"Oh, that's easy. Him," and she pointed to the tall, black one. Sean clapped his hand over his mouth, but his green eyes snapped with glee.

"Him? You serious?" The old man took off his beat up Stetson and scratched his wild mass of white hair.

"His name is 'Freedom'. I named him weeks ago when I first found him." Cass put her arm around the horse's head and hugged him possessively.

"Hmmm. Okay, I'll have him in the main stable for you tomorrow. The day after, we get to work. See you in the morning," and he marched off toward the compound shaking his head.

Nearing the house, Cass and Sean spied Matt on his hands and knees doing something to the lawn. About four yards away, hands on hips, stood his father, glaring down at his son. "No! Not that way. You have to loosen the soil underneath before you replace the sod."

"Ewww, Crikey! Let's go around the other way. Matt's in the shit again."

"Sean, watch your tongue," Cass hissed, trying not to laugh.

CHAPTER SEVEN

"Cassy," Sean began in a quiet, thoughtful voice, "why did you pick Pine Image? Why didn't you pick one that you can show, like, at the Denton Fair, and Ft. Worth and stuff? He's no show horse," he sneered. "What classes could you put him in? Even in Equitation he'd be a freak! He's so big and black and stuff." He scuffed his boots through thick Bermuda grass, head down. Three dogs followed them patiently—two blue-eyed beauties—and Stray, who was the alert one, and whose steps were springing with the pure joy of living.

"His name is Freedom—that's the name I picked for the horse poster Big Sal put up on my wall at Haven House. I looked at him and that's what I felt. Freedom." Cass smiled dreamily, remembering, never thinking the day would come when she would have a real, live horse called Freedom. Bagpipes screeched out "Danny Boy." Suppertime; the horses were exercised, groomed and fed. Now it was time to relax. School tomorrow and that meant Pat and Earl would be working with her and Freedom in the morning. Stray whipped around her, happily begging for attention. Cass rubbed the silky black ears as he stretched up to her chest, and she received a complete facial licking in response.

Laughing, they continued toward the house.

"Hey, kids, don't forget next Sunday's Easter. First, church, then everyone from all the local churches meets for lunch at the hall, as usual," Meg called out to them as she rounded the corner of the house, heading for the back entrance.

Stunned, Cass stopped dead in her tracks. *Easter! Church!* Her head whirled at this new mountain to climb. Churches were places you passed going somewhere else. Sometimes breathtaking music caused her to stop and listen.

Wonder what they're doing in there? Someday I'll sneak in and see.

"C'mon," urged Sean. When she didn't move, he turned. "What's the matter? You look funny." Stray whined in agreement.

Walking slowly, head down, Cass was silent. Her head spun with new fears of the unknown. *I'll talk to Bri. She'll tell me what to do. Easter. There's an old song about Easter bonnets. No freaking way will I wear a bonnet covered with flowers and bows. Eeeeewwww!*

Sitting on the bench in the mud room, they struggled out of their boots. The comforting aromas of stables, flowers and pine trees that mingled here, made Cass feel at home. Now church. No question but that she would do what the family did, reminding herself of the special status she had within this wonderful family. Well, except for Matt the Monster. Finally recognizing him as the enemy, her mission focused on finding out why he hated her, so she could try to fix it. Going back to New York was not an option. Ever. That she knew for sure, so she figured the only thing to do was stand up to his bullying. She had nothing to lose by defending herself.

"You going to sit there all day? I'm hungry. Come on."

The door slammed and in stomped Matt. "Earl says you want Pine Image. Are you nuts?" The bench squeaked in protest when his weight flopped down on it.

Cass removed her other boot and banged it against the inside of the wooden box to dislodge the dried mud.

"Nuts? Why do you say that?" Her voice reminded her of Bri, firm and sure. A hint of a smile twitched the corner of her mouth.

Matt's eyebrows shot up in surprise at her comeback. "Well, for one thing, he's sure not an ideal specimen of Quarter Horse, and the Paint part of him looks like an old scar. You're not going to win anything with him. And he's lazy, stupid, too big and the wrong color." His muddy boots were flung into a corner. No secret that he was in a fighting mood. Beating at the dried dirt on his black jeans, he stood, glaring at this know-nothing guttersnipe.

Cass looked him in the eye and slowly lifted her eyebrow; the corner of her mouth twitched — this time she didn't try to hide it.

"Damn it, LeDrew, just who the hell do you think you are?" Shouting now, Matt thumped his fist into the heavy oak door, trying hard not to show he'd hurt his hand.

"Matthew! Apologize to Cass right now and go wash up for supper." Meg had appeared at the door.

Matt murmured, "Sorry," as he passed in front of them.

Meg picked his muddy boots out of the corner, put them on the rack to dry, smiled at Cass, and said, "Coming? We're having chicken fried steak for supper. Kayla makes the best in the South."

She gave Cass a little hug around her waist. "And you, my girl, are going to get a crash course in religion before next Sunday." Laughing, she leaned over and gave Cass a little peck on the cheek.

Aww — that felt so good. Am I supposed to give her one back? Cass ducked her head, overcome by shyness, and a new sensation. It felt good — warm, kind, and promising forever. Turning to Meg, Cass realized that tears blurred her vision. So that Meg wouldn't think she was sad, she sniffed loudly then grinned while the tears spilled over.

"I feel so...so...um, light. Like I'll float away on a cloud of pure joy where there's no fear or unhappiness." Darting a glance at Meg, she murmured, "I think I'm happy here. Y'know?"

Stopping, Meg engulfed her in her special bear hug, swaying with her and laughing in glee. "Of course you are, silly! And we're happy that you're happy here, y'know?" The way Meg copied Cass's words was hilarious, and the mood continued right into the kitchen.

It was Sunday, and everyone was busy with their routine of training horses, yearlings and weanlings for the show circuit. The Rocking K had already made their name as one of the top breeders and trainers of Quarter Horses and Paints, so Pat didn't attend many of the smaller shows. He concentrated on the local one in Denton to give the weanlings and yearlings a chance to get used to crowds and to being transported in trailers. It was a good place for the kids to show their horses and try to get any problems sorted out before Ft. Worth. It was the biggy: the World American Paint Horse Show where everyone goes and enjoys themselves. The horses and riders don't have to qualify with year-round points in order to show there. It's a spectacular place to be whether you compete or just watch.

Matt was silent, giving the impression he was gravely wounded and totally misunderstood. He groomed his horses till they shone, cleaned out their hooves, oiled them, trimmed whiskers from muzzles and ears. Then he clipped the mane off the horse's crest about a foot down its neck. After examining his handiwork, he dug in his bag of goodies and offered each horse a few pieces of chopped apple as he walked each one back to its stall.

He was good. Very good. In the saddle, he became part of the animal: so smooth, graceful and confident. This was his world.

Cass watched his every move, learning, envying, and determined to be the best that she could be. Turning, she ran smack into Pat.

"Whoa up, there, little Cassy. Earl has Pine Image all tacked up and ready to go. Let's go show them how it's done." Together they strolled through the long stable which was a huge, modern structure full of designer stalls, black steel bars and sliding doors. Cass always felt like she'd stepped into a sci-fi movie. Outside they even had a mechanical horse exerciser that looked like a huge wheel on its side with special mesh and springy type fencing around it. The Rocking K had every imaginable piece of equipment with which to aid in the training and well-being of its animals. Mind-boggling stuff to Cass. They stopped now and then to rub a soft muzzle, scratch between the ears and have a little talk to inquisitive and gentle members of the family. This included, of course, the cats and dogs as well as the horses. Continuing on, they passed one of the bigger training paddocks that was encircled with flex-fence. Cass loved the heady aroma of rich hay, wood shavings, and manure mingled with the pungent odors of pine tar and liniment. Pure heaven.

There stood Freedom, black coat gleaming, silvery mane and tail newly shampooed, and sporting a silver-trimmed saddle and bridle. The snowy white patch half way down his side that qualified him as a Paint, gleamed defiantly. To Cass it looked like the State of Texas, lying on its side. Freedom knew he looked good. Putting his nose in the air he trumpeted his satisfaction clear across the valley. Stray pinned his ears back and barked, obviously annoyed at this disturbance.

Cass laughed and walked over to Freedom to stroke his satiny coat. He gently butted her with his head—his way of telling her to climb aboard and let's go. She took a minute to examine the new saddle and bridle—or tack, as she now knew to call it. *Tack! Why tack? How did that word come to mean this stuff? Harness is harness. You harness a horse. But if you're going for a ride, you tack up. Must find out about that—it's bugging me.*

Cass mounted Freedom, gathered the reins loosely in her right hand, then squeezed her knees and calves gently, urging him into a walk. *Totally different than Old Yeller, that's for sure.* She couldn't keep the smile from her face. Taller than Yeller, Freedom held his head a bit higher and took longer strides. At the trot he was like sitting in an easy chair and then—she couldn't resist—she squeezed him into a lope with no effort at all. They were traveling clockwise around the ring and he automatically started into the lope on his proper lead—his inside foreleg reached out first and continued to do so all the way around. Eyes misting, heart thudding with pleasure, Cass was in another world.

"Just a minute, Missy. Have you forgotten *everything?*" Earl strode over to her. Pat stayed in the middle of the ring.

"What have I done?" Cass swung Freedom toward Earl and sat back a bit, putting slight pressure on the horse's mouth. Freedom stopped dead. Her heart was in her mouth; she felt like crying; she was feeling magic just a moment ago.

"You've got to loosen him up first. You don't put him into a lope right off! You want to ruin him?" Black eyes flashed in the dark face, but remained kind beneath the bristly white brows.

"Hold on there, Earl," interrupted Pat. "She knows better but just couldn't wait to try him out, right, Cassy? Some different from the Old Yeller mare, right? Don't blame you a bit. Carry on what you're doing, get the feel of him and let him get used to you." Turning, he whacked his old buddy on the shoulder then gave it a friendly shake. "Thanks, Earl. I know she's in good hands. Bring them along the way you feel is right for them, but—a big but, here—let her play with him for a while today, okay?" He waved at Cass and strode out the gate, Sam and Jesse close behind. Stray looked back at Cass, then at Pat, and made her decision. She stayed in the ring.

"Mr. K's right, you know. You go ahead and play for a while and I'll just rest my old bones." He wandered out the gate to a miniature white grandstand with a white marble water fountain next to it. Sean joined him; he had been out checking the mares with his mother and Bri. Sam and Jesse appeared and lined up beside them on the long, white boards, panted and watched every move of horse and rider. Obviously Sam and Jesse figured this would be more exciting than whatever Mr. K. was up to. Stray stood her ground in the ring.

Cass grinned at the picture they made; inside she felt the thrill of independence. What she commanded the horse to do, he did. If she didn't do it properly, he messed up. Like Earl kept reminding her, she had to ride with her mind. It was all up to her, and her alone. Excitement and determination rushed through her body — because she knew she could do it.

"Okay. Now do all the figures you did on Yeller. Remember to check for the right leads in the figure eight. Don't forget to stop when you're done. Don't let him move. Do your quarter turns, then back up six steps, stop, walk forward six steps and stop. No fidgeting."

Cass nodded and began the figures, drilled into her brain by working with Old Yeller under the eye of Mr. K and Bri. The big push came with Earl. But the difference! Cass barely moved in the saddle. When asked to change leads, Freedom became a well-oiled machine. She'd lean a bit; he'd turn in that direction. Cool! She wished her mother could see this. Out of the blue that thought sprang into her mind. No word from her at all. Cass suddenly felt cold and distracted.

"Try him with some reining, you know, like Dad and I do with the two we're taking to Ft. Worth." Apparently Matt had become tired of playing the martyr and had come to watch.

"Yeah, right. You know darn well I don't know anything about reining." Cass loped over to the gate and stepped off. The horse stopped dead. *Wow! That was too cool. Just like the real cowboys do.* Grinning at her inner pat on the back, she tossed the reins to Matt, who was leaning over the top of the gate.

"Show me how it's done, big guy." She couldn't believe she'd just repeated a sexy line from a recent TV show. Stifling a giggle, she slipped through the gate and sat with the others. Actually, she sat beside Stray who immediately washed her face then tried to curl up on her lap.

"Quit that. Sit!" Stray sat. Those watching raised their eyebrows in surprise. Stray had obeyed a command—a minor miracle.

"How did you do that?" demanded Sean.

"He's smarter than he looks. He picked that up after just a couple of tries—and can do lots more if you treat him right." Cass turned her attention to the ring. "Look!"

Matt was aboard Freedom, doing figures of eight and getting along fine. He decided to bring the horse to a halt, stand, then back up six steps and halt. Then walk forward six steps, halt, swing quickly to the right, then...and that's where it all fell apart. As Freedom was going through his paces, his feet dragged slower and slower, his head drooped lower and his tail clamped down tight. He almost sat in the dirt when Matt tried to make him back up.

"Jeez, girl, you've ruined him already!" With that he yanked Freedom around and put him into a lope. Half way around the ring, he dug him with his right heel, sat back, leaned left and pulled the horse's head left. Freedom made the turn in his own good time, slowed to a jog and headed for the gate.

Everyone laughed except Matt. He was flushed red to the tips of his ears, but held his temper. In fact he took it a step further. Grinning, he dismounted and turned to Cass.

"Can't believe it. He's plain lazy, just as we thought. But you're doing real fine, Cass. I'll find you a horse you can show at Denton, though, no problem." Looping the reins over the top rail, he waved and ambled up the path to the stables.

This sudden show of interest and understanding stunned them. Cass took it all in, wondering what he was really up to.

She hadn't quite conquered "trust" yet, and doubted she'd ever lose that keen wariness that had saved her so often in New York.

Walking back to the stable, followed by Earl and Freedom, Cass asked Sean where Bri was.

"Aw, she and Mom were having another of their 'little differences', as Mom calls them. They don't yell, so it's not a fight, exactly. But, like Dad says, they're like a couple of spitting cats." He laughed, kicked at a pebble and said, "Maybe it'd be better if they just let loose and get it over with, y'know?" Cass thought those were wise words for a kid. She was glad they didn't fight. Yelling always upset her whether she was involved or not.

"I've heard them a couple of times, but when I asked Bri if anything was wrong, she just said 'same old, same old' and that was it."

"Most of the time it's because she wants to go out with the gang into Denton, like, to a movie or something. Mom says she's too young."

Freedom was hooked onto the hot-walker when they reached the stables. Head down, he plodded along as the big iron spoke led him around in circles. When he cooled out enough, he would be given a drink of water, groomed and let out into the pasture for the night.

"It's okay, Earl, we'll look after him and turn him out if you like."

"Well, great. If you can stay and help out, we'll all get home for supper early."

"There's something I'd like to ask you, but I don't want you to get mad at me." Cass looked up into those sparkling black eyes; so familiar; so beautiful.

"Go ahead, ask. You'll never learn anything if you don't ask. You got to always ask 'why' and make sure you get an answer." He grinned at her, his dark wrinkled face framed by the neat white beard, a picture of patience.

"Am I going to make a fool of myself by trying to show Freedom so soon?"

"Cassy, even the most experienced riders make fools of themselves from time to time. It's all part of sports—any sports. You'll goof sometimes no matter how good you are or how much you're paid. You'll have fun, and that's the truth."

Earl took hold of Freedom's halter and slowly rubbed the big gelding's head, scratching between the ears and talking soft and low. He looked up, took a deep breath and said, "Cass?"

"Yeah?"

He tipped his battered hat forward, scratched his curly white head, and announced, "He's bored."

"Who?" Cass was confused.

"Your horse."

CHAPTER EIGHT

"Aw, Mom, give it a rest." Bri strode off the patio and smacked into Cass as she rounded the corner. Yelps of alarm ended in laughter, and they walked away together toward the woods.

"Um...how was school today?" Cass waited. No answer. "Wish I could go to school, but using your books sure helps." Silence. "I couldn't help overhearing what you said back there. Are you okay?" Concern for her friend was genuine, and Bri knew that. Reaching out, she hung her arm around Cass's neck and hugged her.

"Yeah, sure I'm okay. I just wish Mom would chill. She thinks I'm still ten years old, I swear! I'm almost 16. My birthday's June 1st; I've got my driver's ed certificate—all that stuff. Some of my friends have their license but can only have two kids in the car with them and have to be off the road at midnight. One guy, Chris, is eighteen so he can do what he wants. Mom freaks if she thinks I'm in a car with those kids. Look—I'm responsible for lots of ranch work. Dad's teaching me to do the books. Still I can't go in to Auburn or Denton with my friends. If I need clothes or stuff, Mom comes with me. I take my driver's test on my birthday, but I'll have to have an adult in the car with me for six whole months. A real bummer. I've been driving here on the ranch since I was twelve, for Pete's sake. But can I drive into town by myself? Noooooo!" Her anger grew with each word until she punctuated her frustration by kicking a solid pine tree trunk. "Oooo! Jeez, I broke my foot."

Cass laughed, knelt and tried to pull Bri's boot off. "You're unglued, big time. What's really wrong?" One more heave got the boot off and another yelp from Bri.

"Is it broken?" She wiggled her toes. "Nope. Never kick solid objects. I've just learned a lesson." Bri grinned at Cass and put her boot back on.

"I already knew that."

"What do you mean by 'really wrong'? I told you what was wrong. I can't take it anymore. I have to wait two more years before I graduate and get out on my own." Limping to the bench under the pines, Bri flopped down.

Cass's mind was in a whirl. All this upset because of movies and parties with friends? Can't take the car to town by herself? Hello?

"You're looking at me funny. What's your problem?" Now Bri was snapping at Cass.

"Um...it's just ...I don't know what...how..." Cass scuffed at the path with the toe of her boot. "I'm like, trying to figure out what the problem is. I know it must be something awful to make you so darn shitty." Finally she lifted her head and looked Bri squarely in the eye. "Listen up, Briana. At least you've got a mother to argue with. She wants to keep you safe. She loves you. Same goes for your father and brothers. Your brothers don't show it, but your father and mother do." Standing, her voice raised, tears streaming down her face, her parting words were, "Why don't you put some of that 'tude into thanking God, or whoever's up there, that you've got a family? Yours seems okay to me, but what do I know? A stinkin' street kid, right? Well, you sound *worse* than one right now. Bitching just because you can't get your own way. Jeez, Bri! Where's your head?"

Heart pounding, fighting back tears of frustration and anger at her friend's blindness, Cass strode back up the path. Things were falling apart. Fear was starting to sniggle into her heart again. She should have kept her mouth shut. Bri was so blind to everything around her. Sure, maybe everything wasn't perfect, but maybe Bri should spend a month in the real world — Haven House, even — before she tramped all over her family. Matt, too. Neither of them knows how good they have it.

"Where're you off to in such a hurry?" Matt was saddling Zipper, an all-around champion. A glistening rich bay color, he pricked up saucy ears as Cass approached then reached out to nibble her sleeve, nostrils flaring with each breath. Stroking his soft muzzle was like stroking velvet. Cass's warning flag shot up. She didn't know why, but she sure had learned to heed it.

"I've got to work Free. Gotta go." She stalked purposefully to the ring where Earl was adjusting the girth. She could hear Matt and Zip following her.

Not until they were all in the ring did Matt drop his little bomb.

"Here. Hop aboard ol' Zip. He's tops at reining, and I'll tell you how to handle him." He looked wide-eyed and innocent at Cass.

How stupid does he think I am? I've heard them talking about this horse. Champion, yes. Hell on wheels, yes! It hurt to know that he didn't care what happened to her. To her knowledge, she hadn't done anything to make him hate her. But he did — big time. Taking a deep breath, she swore that he wouldn't wreck her dreams, or make her feel like a piece of crap. Not anymore.

"Sounds like a good idea, Matt. That way I'd get the feel for what I'm supposed to do with Free." Smiling brightly she added, "But you get on first and show me how it's done."

A tiny grin appeared beneath Earl's bushy white moustache, and a twinkle appeared in his hooded eyes. He led Freedom out of the ring, shut the gate and leaned on the upper rail, waiting.

After much urging to the point of bullying by Matt, Cass finally apologized for wasting his time, stating that she just wasn't ready to ride such a spirited horse.

"I hope you understand, Matt. Someday maybe, but not today." Smiling sweetly she left the ring.

With a heart-felt curse, Matt jumped on Zipper, jerked him around and spurred him down the ring just as his father approached, scowling and gritting his teeth. He stopped beside Cass.

"Why's Zip out?"

Cass's explanation was met with silence. Her gut immediately tied itself into knots and she could actually feel her heart thudding against her ribs. *Oh, Mr. K, don't send me away. I didn't have anything to do with this!* Sweat trickled between her breasts, leaving a tell-tale wet patch. *Dammit! I'm through begging. I won't do it. If he says go – I'm history. I can take care of myself.* With determination, Cass reached back and retied the leather shoelace that held her hair.

"By the way, Cass, if you don't mind, could you call us something other than Mister and Missus Kiley? It gives us the creeps. Makes us feel old." He grinned down at her from his towering six foot four, and she began to relax. A breathless kind of warmth crept into her soul.

Cass nodded slowly, and with a small smile asked, "What should I call you?"

"Oh, I don't know. You can call us Grandma and Grandpa if you want."

"But that sounds so *ancient!*" Cass replied with horror.

Pat threw back his head and laughed. "I guess maybe it

does, but you already have a Mom, so that's out. How about just calling us by our first names?"

"No!" Her mind whirled but no names suited how she felt about them. They were more than a name to her; they were a feeling, an emotion. Looking up into Mr. K's big blue eyes she whispered, "Um...you don't understand. You see...ah...you're not just a name, like, you're part of me and...it's something I can't explain. You know what I mean?" Cass asked hopefully.

"Well, yeah, I think I do," Mr. K murmured, head down, eyes blinking.

"Can I call you Poppa?" It was just a whisper. Her eyes were closed. She held her breath.

Big, warm arms wrapped around her, hugging, rocking and a quavering voice murmured, "I'd like that a whole lot, Cassy."

"Would Mrs. K mind being Momma?" She quickly added, "I don't mean Mama, like mother, but Momma." She paused while looking toward the house. "She's always there, so warm, so...well...everything."

Breaking the emotional tangle they'd woven, Pat held her at arms length and announced formally to Cass that he and Meg were her Momma and Poppa from here on and forever.

"Keep your damn feet still!" The shout from the ring was like the crack of a rifle. "Whoa! Stand!" The sharp commands only made Zipper more skittish. He shuffled, tossed his head trying to get relief from the strangle hold Matt had on the reins, and ended up spinning on his hind legs, shaking his head wildly.

Pat strode into the ring, commanding calmly but firmly for Matt to get off the horse. Now. Ignoring his father, Matt put the spurs to Zip. That was the last straw for poor Zipper. He spun, bucked vigorously twice, and Matt flew through the air, landing in a crashing heap at his father's feet. Zip stood stock still, stared at Matt, and snorted his disgust.

"Name of God, Matt, what do you think you're doing?

That's an eighty thousand dollar horse you're messing with!" He stomped back and forth, almost frothing at the mouth, not even noticing Earl quietly led Zip away. "Say something, damn it! What're you trying to prove here? Have you lost your bloody mind? Get on your feet and go look after your horse, or are you going to bugger that up, too? Keep this up, boy, and it's back to basics for you. I can't have you ruining what I've spent a lifetime building for us, you hear me, Matt?" He spun around in frustration, beating his hat against his leg. "His mouth is bleeding; you spurred bloody holes in him. That's cruelty, and I won't have it! You look after him real good, you hear me? No scars! No white hairs!" Taking a deep breath, he quietly murmured, "Jesus, Matt, don't do this to us. I just don't know who you are anymore."

Matt watched his father walk away, slowly shaking his head, shoulders slumped. He wiped his face with grimy hands then painfully struggled to his feet, and looked around.

They had all left.

He was alone.

CHAPTER NINE

After an uncomfortable supper, eaten mostly in silence, Cass felt at a loss. She found herself switching her head into neutral by trying to name all the flowers that were in her unobstructed view left by Matt's no-show. Swallowing Kayla's gourmet dinner was a chore. Her taste buds had deserted her. One more mouthful would make her puke. Excusing herself, she bolted through the patio door and down the white cobbled pathway.

Now what? Had she completely lost touch with the family?

Going to the stables had to be avoided in case Matt had gone into hiding there. Hanging around with Bri wasn't an option. Cass had never seen her so unapproachable. Perhaps she should have just kept her mouth shut. But what she said was the truth.

Wandering through the maze of fragrant floral artistry, she found Mrs. K, er, Momma who also appeared to have escaped from the unpleasant supper table into the midst of her prize rose arbors.

"Hi, Mrs...ah...Hi! Want some help?" Cass just couldn't come out with the new aliases, even though she loved the names as much as she loved the people they belonged to. Such a good feeling. She wondered about the kids on her block back in New York. When she thought about them now, she could pick out the survivors, hoping some of them would make it out of there to someplace like this, where they felt wanted.

Laughing and shaking her head, Meg asked, "Having trouble with the Momma bit? I, for one, love it. Especially with your accent. *Mawma*." Bending over she reached for a pale pink and yellow rose that had seen better days. She nipped it off with a pair of red pruning shears. All her gardening tools were red so she could spot them when she forgot where she'd laid them down. Just from rustling through the blooms, the sweet aroma of roses exploded into the air. Cass reached and cupped one cream-and-pink bud in her hand, then quickly snatched it back, sucking where a thorn had stabbed her finger. It tasted salty.

"Did one of my beauties bite you?" Momma laughed. "Here. You're younger than I am. Climb up on the trellis and clip off those three dead clematis like a good girl?"

"Sure!" Stuffing the pruners into the back of her jeans, Cass scrambled to the top, had the offending blooms snipped and stuffed down the front of her green polo shirt and climbed down before Meg had reached the padded bench in the gazebo.

"Good Lord, child, don't you do *anything* at a normal pace? Come sit with me. I have a thermos of iced tea with lemon and sugar." She poured two big glasses, added a slice of lemon and a straw, and sat back. "Take the pruners out of your pocket before you get another wound."

"Thanks," murmured Cass, and sat across from her on a matching chair, laying the pruners gently on the glass table top.

"Why do you work so hard in this heat? I know the ranch hands do your gardening and stuff. Don't they do this?"

"Oh, heavens yes! I couldn't begin to keep this place looking decent, but just to putter around is so relaxing. I find myself thinking over problems more clearly out here and at the same time feel rejuvenated—you know, new energy." Meg brushed at some dirt on her shirt—actually it was Pat's, as were the worn out khaki shorts. Neither fit, but served as her gardening uniform. She felt at peace when wearing them.

"It's so beautiful here. I sometimes find myself trying to compare it to where I used to live, and I can't. It's like, too different, a whole other planet." Cass paused then added, "Even the people. It's hard to believe, let alone understand. I just wish..."

Meg sipped the iced tea, swirled the ice cubes around, waiting.

"You just wish what, Cassy?"

"School. I'm afraid I'll never get to go back and there's so much I want to learn and do." Shrugging her shoulders shyly she added, "I'd like to be a vet someday."

"And why shouldn't you be? Believe in yourself, work hard and you'll be whatever you choose to be. Life is full of choices: right, wrong, hate, love, good or evil. It's not always easy. Sometimes we have to compromise, but it all comes down to believing in yourself." Setting her glass carefully on a paper napkin to sop up the drips, Meg looked Cass right in the eyes, their deep green enhanced by her bright green shirt.

"Can I ask you something, Cassy?"

"Sure." Her surprise reflected in her voice.

"It's Brianna. She's unhappy. Whatever it is goes deeper than just being angry because we won't let her run loose in town." A frown drew her beautifully arched brows down; her eyes clouded. "Has she said anything to you that might shed some light on what this is really all about? Poppa and I have racked our brains over this and can't come up with a thing. She's doing well at school; her horses are coming along fine for the Denton show..." shaking her head, she half-whispered, "Oh, God, I wish ...I hope she's okay."

This was a first for Meg and Cass, to really have a heart-to-heart. Oh, they chatted all the time but never really talked. Cass discovered she wasn't the least bit shy about saying what was on her mind. How times had changed!

"I sort of raked her over pretty good yesterday. I got fed up with her moaning about movies, parties and driving. I told her she didn't know how good she had it, and stuff like that." Cass looked over at Meg and bit her lower lip. "She hasn't talked to me since."

"Hmm. Well, I wouldn't worry about it, Cass. Maybe that's what she needed: a blast from someone her own age."

"You know what I really think, Momma? She's just antsy, like, you know, with exams coming soon, her first prom, who she'll go with, what she'll wear. You know—girl stuff. I've heard her on the phone with Shawna. That's all they talk about." Cass took a big gulp of iced tea, shivered as the tart lemon connected with her taste buds, then continued. It all had to be said. "The Denton show is about two months away. It's just as important to her as Ft. Worth and Houston, and, yeah, Oklahoma City. Bri and I clean tack, groom, clean and oil hooves already! She's choosing outfits for different classes she's showing in, digging out the show halters with the silver on them, you know? Isn't it kind of early? Uh, speaking of tack, I can't figure how saddles and stuff get to be called tack. I put stuff on the wall with tacks…it sure beats me!" She loved every minute of this, and thought how her own mother might have enjoyed it, too. But maybe not. She didn't want to think about that right now.

Meg put her head back and burst into a throaty, contagious laugh, reached over and squeezed Cass's hand. "Girl, you're a gem, a real gem. Always asking questions."

"Oh, I don't mean to bother you with things. I'm sorry…"

"No, no! Quite the opposite—I love it! And to answer your question the word tack comes from *tackle*. It means the gear you need for sports like fishing and riding. Tack is just the shortened form of the word."

Checking her watch, Meg remembered she needed to make a phone call, and would see her later. "And thanks for the chat! Remind me this evening to hunt up a couple of books I think you'd enjoy. They're full of facts, trivia, that sort of thing, okay?"

"That would be great! Thanks, Momma!" Smiling broadly and feeling relaxed, Cass wandered through the sweet scented gardens and into the cool shade of the majestic pines.

Deep in thought, scuffing through the fallen pine needles on the path, she realized there were so many things that had no answers. Like—where will she go at the end of the summer? The first of August school registration took place. How could that work with no parent to register her? I hope Mom will write soon.

Sighing, she felt the old familiar heaviness return to her heart. Her stomach knotted. No matter how good things were now, this temporary dreamland would soon be part of her past. That's what kept her from letting herself go, from letting herself be the person she knew lay waiting within. Maybe someday...

"Matt!" Cass tripped over his feet. Dressed all in black, as usual, he sat with his head in his hands, on the bench under the old pine. "You scared me!"

Slowly he lifted his head, and focused his eyes on her.

"Hi," he said quietly. With his dark hair falling almost to his eyes, and his face as pale and drawn as if suffering intense pain, Cass could only stare at him. Who was this stranger?

With a start, she remembered the terrible fall he had taken from Zipper.

"Are you all right? Are you hurt?"

"No. I'm okay, thanks." Gone were the animosity, sneering and rudeness of the Matt she knew. It threw her off balance— for the moment. She didn't trust him. Still, she had to say something.

"Um, Matt...I'm...sorry about that blowup in the ring.

I...hope it wasn't anything I said or did that, like, made you mad." Cass's voice faded at the end as she slowly turned to retrace her steps.

"Wait. Please." Leaning against the back of the bench, Matt put his head back and rubbed his face vigorously.

"Shit!" The disgust in his voice stopped Cass in her tracks. She turned toward him, afraid of what was coming next. He didn't sound like he might explode, but...

"I'm so sorry, Cassy." He shook his head in misery; stringy black curls met his furrowed brows. Long-lashed lids covered the deep blue of his eyes.

"It's okay, Matt. I know something's bugging you."

"Yeah." Standing abruptly, he paced in front of the bench, eventually stopping in front of her. "I don't know what's wrong with me. I wish I could lose the crappy feelings. Like, they're boiling all the time, y'know?" His eyes were cloudy. His brows shot up, uncertain, and begging for understanding.

"Aw, Cass. I shouldn't lay this crap on you. You don't know about stuff like this." He sank back onto the bench, elbows on his knees, and head hanging — again.

Cass bristled. *No, Cass, hold your tongue. Don't interfere. Remember. Bri isn't speaking to you now. But what does this spoiled rich brat know about feelings? Nada, zip, zilch.*

She erupted.

"Listen up, boyo! Stop feeling so bloody sorry for yourself! You want crappy feelings? You want boiling? Come with me. You wouldn't last one week where I come from. Not even one day." Her anger spewed like lava. She saw confusion on Matt's face, but she couldn't stop.

"Yeah, you're screwed up big time! You're not doing anything about it! Money, a car, or strutting your sorry ass around Columbus doesn't seem to fix it. You'll still be dissin' your folks about something. So quit it. Stop right now." Cass plunked down beside him and grabbed his hand. "Smarten up, Matt. If I can survive for fifteen freaking years, practically on my own with a big, fat nothing, *you* can survive without all the crap you keep whining that you need. You want all the latest styles and your own sports car just so you can look good. You're family is getting it right in the gut over you, you selfish lump of horseshit."

Cass put her face right in his and whispered, "You've got it all, Matthew Kiley, even a Family Tree you seem so damn proud of. So *earn* that branch with your name on it. Wake up. Look around and start seeing what you could *do* and *be*—anything you want. Just be yourself. You might like who you find. I know I might like you better."

His eyes squeezed shut.

Tears ran down his face.

He didn't see her leave.

CHAPTER TEN

"Time for a family barbecue. What do you say, gang? Here Matt, grab some bacon and pass it on." Pat handed the platters around as Kayla brought more from the kitchen.

"Awwwwright! When?" Sean was always up for any kind of festivities.

"Saturday afternoon. Sal's coming home for Easter, so it's a good time to get together. Sound okay?" Sparkling blue eyes swept the table. "Any objectors?" Grinning, he tackled his bacon and eggs.

"That's great! I haven't seen Aunt Sal for ages. I want to show her how big Shania is and how she handles." Bri flushed with anticipation. "How long can she stay?"

"I'm not sure," replied Meg. "I know she plans to be here Friday sometime and will probably stay over Easter Monday."

Matt silently pushed the food around on his plate. The past ten days he'd been fighting his own private battle. Confused, angry, ashamed — he could barely function.

"Can we have pizza, too? Please?" Sean begged.

"I think you're part Italian," laughed Meg.

Cass held her breath. *Big Sal! Coming here!* She squirmed with an icy clutch of dread, which worked itself into a shiver of excitement.

Too loud, she blurted, "Where's she staying?" Cass wasn't sure she wanted Sal under the same roof with her. She didn't want even a tiny reminder of Haven House to spoil her little corner of heaven.

"With her folks near Oak Point, just south of here. Cass, one of these days we should go visiting so you don't think we're anti-social." Bri was actually talking to her normally. Thank goodness! Cass relaxed a bit and began to eat her breakfast. Maybe it will be all right as long as Big Sal wasn't staying in this house. Cass had so many questions for Sal, but wasn't sure she wanted to hear the answers.

"You're frowning, Cass. Got a problem?" Meg stirred milk into her steaming mug of coffee.

"Just thinking. I'm okay, thanks." She didn't look up.

"Honey, it's been almost three months since Sal has seen you or spoken to you. She says she can hardly wait to get here and give you a big hug — then hear all the dirt!"

Cass felt the inner knot disappear as a breath of relief swept over her, lifting her from what was threatening to be a downer right on up to an awesome high.

"She said that?" Her face felt hot, and the imported Scotch marmalade on her toast took on a tangy flavor she'd never noticed before. Heart thumping, she continued, "Will she have time to see me ride? Or at least to see Freedom?"

"Of course! We'd have to fight to keep her away from here." Laughing, she said, "I think Sal will be over the moon when she sees what you're doing around here. We're so proud of you, Cassy."

A lump lodged in Cass's throat, not allowing her to speak, so she just nodded, smiled, and reached for her juice.

"Okay. Plans." Pat put both large, tanned hands flat on the

tablecloth, which signaled that he meant business. Everyone paid attention.

"Your Mom, Matt and I have to go to Ft. Worth on horse business. We're leaving tomorrow morning, early, and don't expect to be back before Wednesday noon. Then there's Good Friday, Saturday's barbecue, then Easter Sunday." He paused and looked around at the family. "Clear?" When they all nodded, he continued. "Kayla and Joshua have their orders so they'll be busy with the day-to-day stuff plus preparing for the barbecue. Anything comes up, I'll have my cell phone with me. We'll be staying at the Marriott, downtown. Now, are there any questions or are all systems go?"

Everyone spoke at once, but the bottom line seemed to be one of agreement.

"All systems are go," mimicked Sean. "May I be excused, please?" He was already out of his chair.

"Where are you off to, Sean? I want to discuss Easter Sunday."

"Aw, Mom, I know all about Easter and stuff. Can't I go help Earl with the mares? He's got to bring them in one by one, even the ones with foals, to check 'em over, do their hooves and stuff. I told him I'd help. Want to come, Cassy?"

"Sean, I want to talk to Cass. You run along and she'll catch up later if she wants to, okay?" Meg's bright smile sent him scampering out of the room and within seconds the back door slammed.

"Well. So much for family conferences. But he's right. He knows the drill."

"So do I. May I be excused please?" This murmured request came from Matt, who hadn't spoken till now.

"Certainly, honey. Have you all your things together for Ft. Worth? We'll be out of here after an early breakfast—about 8. I've okayed it with school."

"Right, Mom. I'll be ready." His slow footsteps could be heard on the stairs, obviously heading for his room.

"Poor Matt. I wish I could wave a magic wand," his mother sighed.

"He'll be okay, Mom." Running her fingers through her still-wet hair, Bri finished her milk then asked, "Now, what about Easter?"

"Simple. Cass has never been to church. She doesn't know much about religion." Meg grinned at Cass. "Where do you want to start?"

"Mom! We're not going to do a rerun on the history of religion *now*, are we?" Bri was alarmed.

Cass butted in with, "All I want to know right now is what to wear and what happens inside your church. Remember, church wasn't big at my house." Cass glanced at Bri, reminding her that a few short months ago she was trapped in a dilapidated concrete jungle—a small corner of a fabulous city which she never got to see. Maybe someday she'd see it for what it really is, and be proud.

"Right. I forgot—it seems like you've always been here."

"Okay. Clothes. I'd like to see you in that sea green outfit we got in Denton. With your beige sandals, choker and ear rings." Meg arched her brows questioningly.

"That's it?" Cass didn't sound convinced.

"Yes. Why? What did you expect?"

"Well…um…I read one time about flowery hats, flowing dresses, high heels and white gloves…" She glanced swiftly at each of the family still at the table.

They're trying not to laugh! What did I say? I'm positive that's what I read!

"You're absolutely right, hon, but that was a long time ago. Mind you, in some places it's still like that. You're more likely to see that stuff at the Kentucky Derby than at church on Easter Sunday these days." Finally the laughter burst forth, and this time Cass joined in, understanding the reason for it.

"Sweet little Cassy." Pat smiled softly. "You've come such a long way since the first of the year that we forget about all that went before. Shame on us."

"No, Poppa, no! I have all of you now." On impulse she rose out of her chair and gave each of them a hug. "Now tell me what goes on inside this church of yours. Do I have to do or say anything?"

"No, nothing like that. We have what we call a family pew. A pew is just a long bench—not a bad smell," Everyone chuckled. "—with soft padding on it, and a padded kneeling board for when we pray. You'll have a prayer book to follow the service and the hymns we sing. Just follow what we do. It's really quite beautiful, Cass. You just relax and look at all the people. You'll know quite a few of them because this is a fairly small community." Pausing for a sip of coffee, she continued. "Afterward the whole lot of us from all the churches goes for lunch at the Community Center."

"That's it? That's what religion is all about? Just praying and singing on Sundays?"

"Heavens no!" Pat turned to Bri. "Remember that book we gave you years ago called *Bible Stories* or something like that? Do you still have it?"

"Sure I do. That's a great idea. Then Cass can get an idea of the people and the time and place of the beginnings of religion. I know right where it is." Bri was on her feet and heading for her room in a heartbeat.

"Religion is basically the belief of God as our maker: kindness, giving, love for all people, knowing right from wrong—that sort of thing." He shook his head sadly. "Unfortunately, this isn't a perfect world, and not everyone believes or cares about anything but themselves. Just look at the news on TV. That tells it all. But if we all try harder, maybe we can make a difference some day. And that's the briefest explanation I've ever heard about the most complex situation on this planet!" Grinning, he reached over and mussed Cass's hair. "Not only that; there are many, many religions all over the world that seem totally different from ours. But basically, we're all human beings, believing in a Superior Being, and only wanting peace. Of course, there are always a few in every religion, and every walk of life that want to stir up trouble, and we deal with it as we must." Pat looked sad as he stated that sorry fact of life.

"Now, Pat, don't start!" his wife pleaded, holding his hand. "Sometimes I think he should have been a preacher."

Laughing, Cass admitted that she had herself in a real panic about church.

"You should have said something sooner." Meg gave her head a little shake. "I should have picked up on your mood. Must be getting old."

"Truth is I didn't *want* to know. Especially if we had to go shopping for a ridiculous dress and a hat that looks like that fruit bowl over there."

"Did you get it all straightened out? The church thing?" Sean busily brushed one of the foals who wasn't particularly enjoying the procedure. Earl was doing the same with the mare. Sean was good with the young stock. He had the patience of a saint, was quiet and confident around them. Not like he was elsewhere, thank goodness, or the horses would be as squirrelly as wild mustangs.

"Sure. Church'll be okay. I'm going to go see Freedom now. Is he in the stable?"

"No. I put him out in the pasture with the others. We'll work with him later, okay?" Earl kept working the rubber currycomb in circles over the mare's slick roan coat, removing loose hairs and giving her skin a massage.

"Sure. See ya!"

Cass felt ten feet tall as she strode long-legged and almost skipping down the lane to the pasture. She had been on a roller-coaster ride with her emotions about so many things lately that it was a relief to be able to just swing along, singing to herself, until she was nearly knocked down by Stray.

"You scared me!" Scolding him, she knelt and gave him a big hug. "Stray, you've got to be the biggest sook in Texas."

Scratching his ears one final time she continued toward the pasture. When she was letting herself through the gate, Stray let out a sharp squeal and took off toward the trees in the corner.

"Stray! Back!" Cass ordered.

The swift black dog stopped, turned to Cass, whining and wanting to keep on going. He was totally upset about something, dashing back and forth in a frenzy.

Cass caught up to him. "What's the matter, fella?" Then she heard strange noises coming from the shaded corner. She stopped. What was it? Weak little squeals. Grunts. Then a muffled shriek and a thump. Cass's heart was in her throat. Should she run for help? What was in there? She wished she knew more about horses—was that a horse making those awful noises?

Stray finally pulled away from her and raced to the corner, barking his head off. He ran back to Cass, still barking, then back to the corner. This time Cass ran after him only to skid to a halt at what she saw.

"Banjo! Oh, no, Banjo!" Grabbing Stray by the collar to get his attention, she pointed to the stables. "Go get Earl! Go! Go!" And Stray streaked away, squirmed under the gate and disappeared up the lane.

Banjo was struggling frantically to get to his feet, but kept falling sideways. His huge brown eyes were ringed with white, his nostrils flared so large that the blood red insides were visible. And he was soaked with sweat and mud. He had been fighting for a long time.

Cass searched in a blind panic for whatever it was that he was caught in, but could find nothing. Instinct threw her to her knees beside the stricken pony and grabbed his halter. Pulling the quivering head into her arms she began to croon to him.

"It's okay, Banjo, it's okay. You'll be all right. Earl's coming. There's a good boy, just settle down..."and she continued quietly soothing him with her voice, stroking his neck and laying her head on his. The old pony slowly stopped struggling, and his breathing quieted. Then he would whimper, go into spasm and then settle a bit. He was in a spasm as Earl and Sean hurtled through the gate, slowing immediately so that Banjo wouldn't be startled.

"Banjo! Jojo — it's me!" Sean made a lunge forward but Earl grabbed his arm.

"No, Sean. Slow. Quiet. He's in a bad way, son, don't upset him. Just go over and keep him quiet while I figure out what's going on." Earl's voice was low and soothing, too, as they approached Cass and Banjo.

"Thank God you're here. He keeps trying to stand, but falls over. He's in pain, I'm sure he is! Look at his eyes and nose! But I couldn't find anything wrong! No loose rope or wire or a snake…nothing!" Heart aching with fright and confusion, Cass started to sob, burying her face in the wet, muddy mane.

Mud and harsh strands of mane ground against her face, and her tears mixed with the strong earth scent and the sharp tang of anguished sweat. *Oh, Banjo, my poor old Banjo. Earl will fix you — he has to! This can't happen — not now — not when everything is so — so — NO. I won't let it.* Cass suddenly clambered to her feet, blinking mud out of her eyes.

"Help me, Earl! We have to get him on his feet! Hurry!" She lunged for the pony's halter.

Earl pulled her gently away from the pony, and held her close.

"No, no. Not right now. You did the right thing, Cassy. Now, you let me go over him and see if I can feel any lumps. He may have hurt himself." Earl's wise, dark eyes were hooded as he slowly shook his head.

The ache in her chest hurt so bad that Cass couldn't move. She knew. Deep inside she knew she was seeing something so natural, and so wondrous that all else ceased to matter. Banjo was making his way out of this world and into a better one. He wasn't struggling anymore; his eyes had lost the wild and confused look; his breathing was softer and slower. *Oh, please, God, don't let him suffer. If you can't make him better, stop his hurting.* It was all she could do to stand there beside Sean and Banjo as Earl ran his huge, comforting hand along the pony's matted side, kneeling close, needing to help but knowing it was out of his hands now. *I want to run. I don't want this to happen. The air even smells different – like lilacs in the schoolyard in New York.* Yes, New York where death, in her memory was always violent, horrible and needless. This was different. Sighing deeply, Cass rubbed her hand over her muddy, tear-streaked face, felt some of the inner pain ease as she realized she was watching peace wrap itself around them.

Sean had wormed his way under Banjo's neck so he could get his arms around it. He murmured to his old friend, petting him, letting his hand gently slip down to Banjo's nose so he would know that his buddy was with him. And Banjo knew. He nickered softly, tried to lift his head, looked at Sean and when their eyes met, Banjo sighed deeply and relaxed into his final sleep.

CHAPTER ELEVEN

The mouth-watering aroma of steaks on hot charcoal, laughter and welcoming shouts trailed Cass down the path where Sean had disappeared into the woods. Knowing Momma and Poppa were eager for her to greet Sal and her family didn't stop her from doing what she wanted—no, *needed*—to do. Be with Sean. Since Banjo's death, he silently wandered through the stables, doing his chores. His eyes told the whole story. Those deep green pools were a mirror to his soul, and his soul was in torment.

She didn't have to go far. Sean had cut through the few trees separating the path from the mares' pasture. Leaning against the fence, gazing through the white flex-fence bars, he didn't move as Cass approached.

"Sean? Can I crash your space or do you want to be alone?"

"Hi, Cassy." The softly spoken words were barely audible.

Silently, Cass stood beside him, looking at the mares and foals, then into the distance. Pecan trees had finally leafed out; rolling hills were spotted with the last of the blue bonnets, the brilliance of Indian paint brush and Mexican hats. Her eyes swam with the quiet majesty, the fresh, slightly sweet smell of nature's offerings which almost took her breath away. How quickly all this had become real and normal to this inner-city girl. She avoided trying to recall exact events of her past; she didn't trust herself. What if the memories made her feel the way she used to? What if they dirtied this clean dream world that was so full of hope? Sure there were problems here—lots of them—but nothing like where to sleep, or would they eat tomorrow, or would they stumble over some poor soul passed out, or dead, in the gutter. Cass prayed that Sean would never experience stuff like that.

"Why did he die?" Sean's muffled words startled her—brought her back to reality and caused her mind to swiftly switch gears.

"Poppa told you the vet said it was probably a heart attack."

"Yeah, I know. But he wasn't sick! I saw him grazing. How come he just up and died?" He looked up at her, his eyes begging her for an answer he could believe, that he would *want* to believe.

Cass closed her eyes tight while her skimpy ranch savvy whirled in her head. What to tell him?

"Um...how old did you say Banjo was? Twenty-five? Twenty-eight?"

"*No!* He was *thirty-two!*" Sean was bristling at her stupidity. "I told you that!"

Good. He was riled.

"Yeah. Sorry about that." Leaning back against the fence and crossing her arms, she looked him in the eye. "That's a very long time for a horse to live, isn't it?"

"It sure is!" Sean answered proudly. "Our horses get the *best* of everything. Banjo was here when my dad was still in school! That's *forever!*"

"Well, don't you think he was getting a little tired? Horses are like people. When they get real old they get tired. That's when they go to heaven, get all better then live forever." Cass hoped she had at least part of the story right. "There are even angels there," she added for good measure.

"You think that's what happened? His heart just got tired and stopped? He isn't sad or anything?" His emerald eyes begged her to agree.

"Yes, I do, Sean. You were there, cuddling him. You heard him say goodbye." Cass's words were soft and convincing, but her heart squeezed at his pain. Sean's chin quivered. He was fighting the tears that would help heal his hurt.

Cass wrapped her arms gently around him. "It's okay. Let the tears out, Sean. You'll feel better." He stiffened in her arms.

"Big boys don't cry!"

"That's wrong! Who told you that? I've seen grown men cry their hearts out, Sean Kiley! They have feelings, too, you know." She hugged him close again. "I'll bet Matt and your dad feel just as bad as you do. Don't forget Banjo's been with them all these years, too. Tears show you loved him and will miss him. You did, didn't you?" The curly red head nodded against her chest, and deep, heartbroken sobs shook his sturdy little body. Cass rocked him gently, whispering, "It's okay, Sean, it's okay." *Now's the time to change the subject.* "I need you desperately, y'know? Like, you show me how to do things the *right* way! I'd still be holding my knife and fork wrong and using my thumb to shovel food onto my spoon. Then there's putting my elbows on the table, coughing without covering my mouth, slamming doors, slurping my juice—do you want me to go on? Oh, what about burping! Gross, eh?" She felt his shoulders relax and shake as he started to chuckle.

Arms around each other they sauntered silently toward the house. The barbecue was in full swing, and the spicy smell of sizzling steak reminded them both that they were hungry.

"Well! Where'd you two get to?" Bri and Matt were walking down the lawn toward the path. "We were hoping you ran away!" They laughed as they met, turned and headed back to the party.

"Hey, little buddy! Wait a minute," Matt's voice was low, and he held Sean's shoulder. "You okay?"

"Yep. Sure am." His red-rimmed eyes were a dead give-away.

"We'll all miss him, Bro, like I miss Sam-the-First. We grew up together and now he's gone. But we love his puppy, Sam, don't we? Maybe Dad will get you another pony." Matt gently pulled Sean closer, tucking him protectively under his arm.

"No. No, I don't think so. There's only one Banjo." Sean stared at the ground for a moment, scuffed the toe of his boot through the grass, then added, "I like what I do now, y'know? Just exercising a couple of horses and helping Earl with the foals. That's where I like being."

"That's cool, Sean, that's cool." Giving him a quick hug, Matt grinned down at his wise little brother.

"Here they are! Come on, you guys—grab a plate and dig in!" Pat was waving a three-foot-long fork in the air and had on an old stained barbecue apron and a beat-up chef's hat. Cass wondered if he knew how silly he looked, then she grinned. He knew *exactly* how he looked—and loved it.

"Cass! Oh, Cassy!" Momma called in a singsong voice from the patio, beckoning her to come. She decided to take her chances with leaving the steak for now and weaved through the small crowd of friends and family who she hadn't met yet.

Surrounding Momma were Sal, an older man and woman, and three younger men—all very tall.

Sal came to her immediately, grasped her shoulders and held her at arms' length, not saying a word for a long moment. Her gray-blue eyes shone with pleasure.

"Look at you, Cassandra LeDrew! I wouldn't have recognized you, and that's the truth. You are one heck of a good-looking filly." Everyone laughed as Sal gave Cass a huge bear hug. "Come meet my family. I've heard that Pat and Meg are keeping you under wraps out here in the boonies, is that right? Well, tonight you'll mingle with the rest of us Denton County yahoos and we'll show you how to *really* party Texas style, right guys?" A chorus of agreement roared out as Sal introduced Cass to her mom (Aunt Jana), her dad (Uncle Mac), and Cousins Joel, Ross and James. "These here are all mine, God love 'em!" Each of Sal's brothers shook Cass's hand and kissed her on the cheek, which was followed by big hugs of welcome from her parents. Such a glowing, happy bunch, Cass thought, not quite able to connect *this* Sal with *that* Big Sal. She could hardly contain herself with excitement. This same woman saved her life! This same woman *gave* her a life!

The gang on the patio, all talking at once, jockeyed for position on the path to the barbecue pit. Plates filled, they settled at one of the many picnic tables laden with every kind of go-withs, vegetables and fruits known to mankind. Sal gave Cass a toss of her head, signaling they should go back to the glass table on the patio. Good idea. They could hear themselves think up there. Off they went.

Comfortably seated, they commented on the mind-blowing music coming from the four friends of James who were gathered by the fish pond, amps cranked up.

"They got to be the best! I mean, like, wow!" Cass was bowled over by this rave-up, as was Sal, truth be known. The steak, fajitas, guacamole, refried beans plus numerous delicious goodies boggled Cass's sense of smell. The mouth-watering aromas completely tuned out the activities surrounding her. She ate. She savored, and ate some more. Then Sal spoke.

"Cass, honey, Mr. Polanski, the grocer at the corner, got in touch with me about the letter you wrote to your mother. At first he didn't know what to do with it because your mom disappeared long before you got hurt. But he knew you, and her, so he opened the letter, recognized Haven House and brought the letter over to me. Of course I put out the word to all the hospitals, clinics and rehab centers in the city. Within two days I was talking to Glenda."

"You were? Honest?" Cass put her fork down. "Um...ah...is she, like, okay?" She wasn't sure she really wanted to know.

"Oh, yes, she's okay, but..." Sal sighed deeply, then looked straight at Cass and laid all the cards on the table. "Cass, your mom is okay, but she's in a permanent care rehab center because, after all the years of drug and alcohol abuse, she's damaged. I think you kids would say her brains are fried."

There was a long pause while Cass let this information sort itself out. Her heart hurt. Her stomach churned.

"Is she in pain? Does she remember me? Like, could I write to her?"

"She's comfortable, but sometimes gets confused. Nothing alarming at this point. Yes, she talked about you all the time I was there, remembering when you were a baby, then a toddler. But it seems to stop there. She's either blocking all the recent years out, or she really has lost that part of her memory. There's no way to tell. But! She wrote you a letter, and I have it in the car. Remind me to give it to you before I go."

"She *wrote* to me? Really?" Not quite understanding why this news should make her feel good, Cass found herself grinning at Sal, her innards settling back to normal. "I'll write her back if that's okay."

"Great! Her address is on the envelope."

They tackled their food in silence for a few minutes before Sal remarked, "The Marauder gang are all in prison. One of those girls died." She didn't look up when she added, "Tony disappeared before they could pick him up."

Cass felt her whole body grow cold.

CHAPTER TWELVE

Red brush; red plastic tipped nylon bristles; long, thick, ash-blonde hair made for a colorful slo-mo image in the mirror as the brush stroked the shiny loose waves, causing single strands to snap and float in the lamplight. Deep blue eyes; sad blue eyes; confused blue eyes with a bewitching slant that enhanced fine, straight brows and high cheekbones. Soft, sculptured lips, which had so recently learned to become a radiant smile remained still and somber. Staring straight at this attractive reflection, Cass did not see herself. Her sight was focused inward.

Mom...I love her...

Sean...He's too young to be so sad.

Tony...Where is he?

Banjo...Why'd he have to die?

Letter...I'm scared to read it.

Sal...Can I trust her? Is she really still the same?

Deep within her entire being, Cass felt tiny cyclones spinning, making breathing difficult. Which painful subject should she face first? Which one did she want to look into clearly and solve, remove, make disappear?

Placing the red brush, now trailing single strands of shining gold hair, back onto the pure white dresser scarf, Cass blinked rapidly a few times, picked up the envelope from her mother, turned off the frosted bulbs that framed the huge white mirror, and lay on her bed. She noticed everything was white or almost-white in her line of vision. The soft cotton of her pajama top was a riot of bright primary colors that intruded on her mood of desolation.

Staring for a long moment at her mother's writing, it was foreign to her. Did someone have to write it for her? Taking a deep breath, she slid her fingernail under the sealed flap, trying to pry it open without ripping the paper. It didn't work, but the blue writing paper fell onto the white bedspread and lay there, daring her to pick it up.

Dear Cassy:

Thank you for your letter. I am happy that you are okay. A lady came here to see me and told me you can ride a horse. Where are you going to keep it? There's no place at home. Your father (this was scratched out). *I wrote my name for the lady. She's going to bring me your picture. I'm going to play bingo now. Goodbye. I love you. Mummy.*

What? She never called her "Mummy"! Cass's mental slam at her mother quickly turned to sadness as she recognized that her mom was really in another world now. In a way this made Cass feel a little better. At least she was being cared for, fed and finding some peace, at long last. But what a waste! After these past months at the ranch, Cass now understood some of what her mother had missed and would never know, and felt the loss. She decided to wait until after church tomorrow to answer.

Her tired mind slid onto the subject of church and she fell asleep on top of the bedspread, clutching the letter.

Sean held her hand tightly as the family joined others heading to the big white church with the tall steeple. The most beautiful music she'd ever heard filled the morning air. Having watched enough TV during the past few months she was quite aware of what she was hearing and seeing. However it was definitely *not* what she was expecting.

Walking up the center aisle with Pat and Meg, greeting friends and neighbors, Cass drank in the rich splendor of the very old, dark oak of the interior. The church was built nearly two hundred years ago. Sun shone through stained glass windows, some showing people from the Bible, others simply set with multi-colored glass segments; no picture, just spectacular color. Below some of them were set brass plaques with engraved words on them. The walls were pure white stucco with oak wainscoting the same height as the pews, and the steps to the altar and the alter floor were carpeted in deep red. Reaching the family pew, Pat knelt, bowed his head, and then stood back while each member of the family did the same. They sat on the dark red cushioned seat. Pat sat last. They all slid onto the kneeling bench, heads bowed. Cass copied their actions.

While the church filled, the huge pipe organ poured its stirring music into every corner, even echoing into the lofty rafters. Cass felt it begin to seep deep within her. She had never felt this way — ever. A sharp elbow alerted her that she was the only one still on her knees. *Just making up for lost time!* She sat back between Meg and Bri.

"Momma," she whispered, "what should I be doing now?"

"From here on you just relax, enjoy, do what we do if you want to, if not, sit back and be happy." Smiling her beautiful smile, Meg took hold of Cass's hand and gave it a squeeze. "Let your mind and spirit free to soar, to soak up the lifeblood of what this is all about. Later you'll have more questions than I can answer."

The choir of harmonized voices began the first hymn, as they filed up the center aisle from the back of the church to the altar. They divided and took seats along both side walls of the altar, singing all the while.

Cass was spellbound. Wonder, beauty and serenity found their way into her slowly healing inner self. Yet nothing unusual was done or said to cause this bewildering sense of self, and of contentment. The all-consuming vibes wrapped around her; she felt, tasted, smelled and heard it. She was completely unaware of those around her. Her mind slid from her mother and her weakness, to Sean and his grief over Banjo. Reflecting on each of them had worried her so deeply, but now she realized that there truly was nothing she could do for any of them except to stay strong, love them, and try to understand.

She would fret about her reaction to the news of Tony later. Disappeared! Jeez!

Suddenly it was over. Chatter grew to a roar as everyone made their way to the parking lot. Back to reality.

"You okay? Did you like that?" Sean was first in line to get her reactions. He looked like a choir boy himself all slicked up and wearing a white shirt, a silk light blue and gray tie and gray slacks. Even his black shoes shone like new pennies. The red curls were just now beginning to show rebellion to whatever he had used to tame them long enough to get through church. The ends were springing up every which way giving him a definitely devilish character, which actually suited him to a tee.

"Not what I expected at all," was Cass's quiet reply.

"You mean you're never going back?" Stopping in his tracks, Sean announced to everyone with ears that Cass was never coming back here again!

The silence was horrible. Guilt squished around within her tummy. He's wrong!

"He's wrong!" she blurted out. "It was all so, so, um…awesome. Yeah. Awesome!" She relaxed at having found the right word, and then added, "I'll be back."

With the after-church catching-up-on-things, conversations began to flow again, and Cass stood with the Kiley family watching Sal's family slowly make their way in their direction. She eyed this approach with mixed emotions. With all her heart and soul she wanted to get Sal alone, to help her understand everything that had happened to her. The big question was if her life before joining the Kileys would make it impossible for her to break free of the unexplainable *things* in her mind. What if she never felt again like she did a short half hour ago? She knew that to feel that way all the time was impossible, but to know that you could, once in a while, would make a person look at things a whole lot differently. *At least it will for me.*

"C'mon you guys, we're off to the Center for lunch. Then we've lots to do before we leave in the morning," Pat called out to them. The boys piled into the cab of the green pick-up that proudly carried the ranch's name and logo on the door, and started off down the lane beside the cemetery. The new buds and blooms were beginning to soften the harsh edges of the centuries-old headstones.

Meg opened the door of her bright blue Grand Cherokee just as Sal arrived.

"You're off so soon?" Sal sounded disappointed.

"Just to the Center for now. We're leaving for Ft. Worth early tomorrow, so there are things to look after."

"That's right. I forgot." Sal walked around the back of the SUV to where Cass stood.

"I wanted to get a chance at another gabfest with you before heading back to New York, but I guess it'll have to wait. Got a call just before we left for church and I have to get back."

Cass felt deep disappointment with a hint of relief. She wanted time to sort some things out in her own mind before she tried to explain what she thought to anyone.

"When will you be back?"

"I'm due for holidays in July, but I never count on those," Sal grinned wryly. "I'll shoot on up here in another month or six weeks. By then you'll have a whole new bunch of info for me to juggle, right?"

"Yeah." Shyly she put her arms out and she and Sal hugged.

"Y'know what?" She asked Sal.

"No. What?"

"Hugs make me feel better."

"You're awful quiet," Sean remarked as he rode Old Yeller beside Cass and Freedom.

"I guess I'm just thinking stuff, y'know. It's so peaceful here among the mares and foals I don't like to spoil it by talking." Leaning sideways, Cass reached Stray's ear when he jumped up, which he did often. "Silly pup! Go run with Jesse and Sam." Stray stayed right where she was.

The easy stride of the horse beneath her, the healthy, heady smell of leather, sweat, green grass and clean, clear air transported Cass into a space that was hers alone. She felt free to think thoughts, plan plans, dream dreams, soar with the mourning doves or just be; this was her private space. Church this morning had opened new doors for her to peek into. A lot of stuff wouldn't be for her, but she knew *some* would. Already she felt better toward her mom, and even thoughts of the unknown tomorrows didn't scare her as much. She would deal with each one in her own way. Cass shook free of her expectations of trying to fix every last worry and problem. Talking to Sal was good; she knew she could say anything to Momma and Poppa. *I trust them but it's hard to stammer out all the things that bother me.*

"Trust," stated Cass out of the blue.

Startled, Sean put Yeller to a trot to catch up. "Did you say 'trust'?" His tanned nose was wrinkled up in puzzlement. The spikes of this morning were covered by his old Stetson.

"Yep, that's what I said." Cass looked across at Sean. "You were teaching me all sorts of things to do and don't do, and all that stuff, right?"

"Right. You did good, too, real quick." He nodded for emphasis.

"You forgot one thing." She waited, but no response.

"Trust."

"Yeah, but that comes when you do all the other stuff right," Sean argued, pulling Yeller to a halt.

"Okay. I guess you're right in a way. How'd you get so smart for a kid? Doing things right gives you a chance to trust yourself and what you're doing and saying, right?"

"Right!"

"Okay. So now I trust *myself.* Now it's time to trust others. I can't go through my whole life not trusting anyone." This time Stray jumped right up onto the saddle with her, nearly gutting herself on the roping horn. Once Cass got her laid across in front of her, with her front feet hanging off her left thigh, she turned to Sean. "What do *you* think? Do you trust yourself?"

A long silence followed by a hesitant, "Well I trust myself to do things I know how to do. I guess it'll take a while before I feel like you do." His voice was quiet and thoughtful. "I didn't have to do the things that you did. That's why you're so far ahead of me."

"That's where you're wrong! You're way ahead of me with *people.* You love and trust most people, and that's *huge!*"

Sean perked up at that, and had to agree with her.

"But I bet you know bad people when you see them."

"No," Cass quietly shook her head, thinking of Tony. "I still have a lot to learn."

CHAPTER THIRTEEN

A squeal of joy followed by Cass's gleeful laughter reached Sean's ears as he bolted out of the house and started down the path to the stables.

"What! What is it?"

"Look at what Earl's doing in the paddock! Look at Freedom! He thinks it's a great game." By this time the two of them were at the fence, watching the performance of the big, tall African-American with his wild white hair, patiently leading a very curious Freedom over poles. They lay flat on the ground in different parts of the paddock. Freedom liked to stop, sniff, shove and nuzzle before he walked daintily over them, looking forward to the next one, just ahead.

"What are you doing that for, Earl? He likes it!" Starting through the paddock gate, Sean was stopped dead in his tracks by an annoyed holler from Bri.

"Sean, get back up here! The bus will be here soon!" A door slammed.

"I don't want to go to school today. I could pretend I'm sick and stay here and watch Earl." His questioning look met Cass's, and Cass was slowly shaking her head.

95

"Not!"

"Aw, c'mon. Just one day won't hurt."

"Sean Kiley, you get your butt up there to the bus. *Now!*" Earl had spoken, and was on the wrong end of a dirty look as Sean spun away and stomped back up to the house. "He sure does hate it when he thinks he's missing something," muttered Earl.

"Okay. Now tell me. What *are* you doing with that poor horse?"

"Hah! 'Poor horse' loves it." Earl and Freedom walked over to meet Cass, and the soft nose twitched back and forth as horse kissed girl. Cass giggled and scratched his forehead.

"This here's the plan, and you've got to listen. Hear me, Cassy?" Earl scowled his business scowl that Cass quickly learned to respect.

"I hear you." What plan? What for?

"We're going to the stable; we're going to put English tack on this horse; *you* are going to learn English style from the bottom up, you hear me?"

Silence. It could be sheer terror at the thought of that tiny bit of leather she had to sit on, or plain old-fashioned excitement. She'd soon know.

"But what'll the folks think? Won't they be mad?"

Earl hadn't waited. The tack in question didn't take up all that much room on a rack in the saddling area, nor did a pair of boots and a white helmet with a leather chin strap. *I think he means business.* Taking a closer look at the strange gear, she told herself that she could do this — no problem. *Can't be any harder than climbing down a broken fire escape at night in the middle of a storm, could it?* This slide into sick humor shot Tony into her thoughts again. *Damn! Would he never disappear from her mind?* She shook her head as if she could dislodge the unpleasant memory, but the dreaded clutch of terror and pain grabbed her. *Oh, please, God, make it go away!*

Taking a deep, steadying breath, Cass walked up to Earl.

"What do you want me to do?"

"Atta girl—itching to get started. Here." He handed her a sheepskin saddle pad and stood back. One look at it and she knew where to put it. It smelled like Bounce, fresh from the laundry. The saddle came next. It felt a lot sturdier than it looked, and had nice knee-rolls on the side flaps to support her knees and legs. The tan leather was so soft she paused to run her hand over it. Amazing. Settling the saddle on the pad, checking there were no wrinkles, she reached beneath the horse's belly, snagged the leather girth and prepared to run the first of two straps through a buckle on the girth. *Hah! I aced this test!*

"Hold it right there," he barked.

Jeez! She stopped short, her heart pounding. *What'd I do?*

"Reach under the front of the saddle pad and snug it up a bit into the under part of the saddle. Then your weight won't tighten it down onto his withers and rub him raw."

"Oh." Cass slowly let out a sigh of relief. *Why do I always overreact?* She knew that the withers were where his neck joined his back. *Fine. I can do that.*

Once the tack was secure and fitted comfortably on Freedom, Cass reached out for the helmet and boots. *I hope no one's looking.* A variety of items including riding apparel were stowed neatly in the huge, rich-smelling tack room. Earl chose items that fit fine—a little adjustment with the helmet so it fit snugly and they were on their way back to the paddock.

"Like I said, you're going to learn to ride English today. Don't get in a panic—it's comfortable. In fact I happen to like it. I'll point out what you'll need to do for each gait, then you just ride around and get used to the feel of it. Got it?"

"What if Freedom doesn't like this saddle?" A dumb question. She didn't wait for an answer and, following Earl's instructions, she was up and on her way around the ring for the first time.

Guiding the horse by gently pulling a rein in the direction

she wanted him to go, they walked around, avoiding the half dozen or so poles that were still on the ground. Cass decided she liked the feel of the English snaffle bit in Freedom's mouth—sort of like a direct line of communication instead of the neck reining of Western riding. Squeezing her lower legs against his sides, she urged Freedom into a trot. Cass immediately began bouncing hard enough to jar her back teeth. Quickly she brought the horse to a halt.

"I don't much like *that!*" she complained to Earl.

"That's because you aren't doing it right. In English you *post.* You rise a bit from the saddle every time his outside front leg steps forward, then ease back down when the leg goes down. But I don't want you to do that yet. You just sit there; find the most comfortable way to sit the trot. Just like Western."

"Why?"

"Why what?"

"Why don't I post, like you said." Cass was sweating in confusion and exertion. There was too much to think about. "Maybe I should put my Tony Lamas on so my feet don't slip through the stirrups. They're so...so...little...weird."

"No way! Those boots could get you hung up so fast it'd make your head spin! These stirrups aren't made for anything but what you got on. Not even sneakers—they slip right through—but lots of people just wear what they want. That's okay until you get into trouble." Earl walked up, checked the length of her stirrups, nodded, checked that the girth hadn't loosened, nodded, and then told her to go back out there until she could sit the trot right.

That took a while. Everything jarred and bounced; her butt would be covered with bruises; her head snapped up and down and her neck hurt. *You get this right, city girl! Relax! That's what Poppa said when I first rode Yeller...relax.* Once she loosened the death-grip her knees had on the saddle she discovered she could go all over the ring at the trot quite comfortably. In fact she aimed Freedom at a pole just to see what he'd do. He hopped over it, headed a bit to the left and repeated the performance over another pole. Cass giggled and encouraged him toward the rest of them. She could *feel* every bulging muscle along his sides and back; she could *feel* him take a deeper breath before he hopped over each pole; she *knew* when he swished his tail or got ready to snort through his flared nostrils! *She was part of her horse!*

Excited and full of wonder she trotted toward Earl. Her face was flushed — she could feel it. Before she could open her mouth, Earl spoke.

"Now, do all that again at the canter. Canter's English. Lope's Western." He strolled away to sit on the bench outside the ring after taking a deep swallow of ice cold water from the marble fountain.

Mouth agape, Cass stared at his retreating back. *Miserable old poop! How about a simple 'good girl' or something!* Totally deflated, she swallowed the lump of disappointment, gritted her teeth and turned Freedom back to the middle of the ring. *I'll show him! I'm not stupid! Jumping'll be easier than hopping over the stupid poles! He'll just hop a little higher. No problem!*

Urging Freedom into a canter, Cass circled the ring once, purposely ignoring Earl's presence on the bench. *I can really feel him move! Love it! No more Western saddles for me!* She turned toward an area where two poles lay parallel to one another and about five or six yards apart. Freedom gathered himself for what was coming — he knew this game already and apparently loved it. The sensation of the power beneath her thrilled her, giving her an inner energy she'd never before experienced. *Go, boy! Atta boy! Up we go!*"

The poles were only about six inches across. They gave the horse a chance to get used to gathering himself and actually jumping over a low object before being asked to attempt the much higher and more difficult jumps in a show ring. Freedom's ears were strained so far forward their tips almost touched; his powerful hindquarters bunched and his front end rose and soared over the first pole. Beautiful — except Cass hadn't expected him to jump so high, and didn't know how to react. *My knees moved! He pulled the reins through my fingers. I can't steer!* It felt like a slow motion movie; first, her butt was almost two feet above the saddle and a foot to the left; her hands clawed in vain for reins that were already threatening to tangle in the horse's front feet; then she simply soared toward the ground. *I'm dead! There's nothing to hold onto. Just sky. No. The fence — I'm going to hit it!* Closing her eyes, Cass landed hard, knocking the breath clear out of her. *Did something wrong...* But Freedom knew exactly what he was doing and kept right on going, repeating the performance which, although picture perfect, was accomplished solo.

Can't breathe...ooow...gasp...oh, my back...it's broken...happened so fast...got to get up...might die if I stay here.

Freedom skidded to a halt, turned and walked back to where Cass, now sitting, chose to leave him. He nudged her helmet with his muzzle. No reaction. He did a repeat, only a little more urgently.

"Leave me alone!" He didn't. This time his nudge shoved her helmet over her eyes.

"Jeez, Dummy! I'm hurt! Let me be!" This time he snorted globs of slobber on her neck, lifted his head and gazed off into the distance.

"Ewww, *gross!*"

Cass didn't know where she hurt worse, her shoulder, her butt or her pride. She could now breathe a bit better, which helped. Being winded a few times in the past, deep breaths were the answer to recovery. But those other times had been from a punch to her stomach. That was different — she got up and ran like stink then. Now she would keel over dead before admitting she was hurting. The glorp from Freedom's runny nose got her moving. Rising unsteadily to her feet, she started to brush herself off when a familiar voice boomed across the ring.

"Remind me sometime to tell you the difference between hopping a pole and *real* jumping." Earl stood up and started toward them. "That's enough for now. Cool him off, clean him and the tack. Later we'll give it another go." As he passed by he added, "Next time you'll get an idea of what you're supposed to do *before* you decide to show off."

Oh, shut your big, fat face!

"I didn't ask him to go that high! That's not fair!" Cass stamped her foot in frustration; Freedom stepped away from her.

"Yer scaring yer horse." Cass hated it when he reverted to barn talk or whatever it was.

"It's okay, Earl, I'm okay. Thanks for asking!" Sarcasm dripped from every word and with her nose in the air she pulled Freedom by the reins and headed for the stable. She strained to hear a reply from Earl. Lucky she wasn't holding her breath.

I've never been so, so, -um...aaarrrgh! Whatever! Stop limping, Cass. Get your nose out of the clouds. Hug Freedom — he looks worried.

When Earl peeked around the end of the stable to make sure all was well, he was greeted with, "Hey, Earl! What time do you want me back here?" He mumbled something and was gone. Cass decided to act as if nothing unusual had happened. Nothing at all.

But just wait till this afternoon. She'd show him!

"Wow! Lookit what Earl's done! Jumps!" Sean's excitement was ballistic.

"Sean! Wait! You've got to change your clothes first!" Bri's orders were ignored, as usual, and Sean dumped his backpack as he raced down the path.

"Sean Kiley, you get back here! I'll tell Mom!"

"Bri! Look!" He was pointing at Freedom carrying Cass effortlessly over a two foot high jump and then continue on to do the same over the next one.

"Crikey! That's a blast! I want to do that!" By this time the red-headed cyclone was standing on the bench beside the ring, hardly able to contain himself. But there was a rule followed by everyone including him. When horses were being trained or worked in either paddock, everyone else switched into a quieter, slower gear as they went about their chores or, in this case, watched. Of course he'd seen jumping before at all the shows they'd attended, but it hadn't occurred to him till just now that it could happen at the Rocking K.

Bri joined him eventually, watching as Cass made a few jumps, returned to Earl, listened as he explained something to her or moved her hands ahead a bit on the reins. Bri was straining to hear everything, Cass noted, and relaxed a bit. She had convinced herself that they'd make fun of her; now it seemed that Bri might want to give it a try. *Don't get too cocky, girl. Wait till Matt sees this.* If he laughed at her for trying something she felt was totally awesome, then Matt would be the loser. He'd love this. He'd be good at it. Maybe, after a while, she'd get him to try it when no one was looking. The reaction of his buddies would worry him, not the family. They always tried weird stuff when the folks went to town.

"Once more around, then I'll have Arthur cool down the horse and look after him. You kids go find branches, logs, poles, weird stuff, and bring it back here. We've got to get him used to jumping anything and everything. Hear me?" Earl stared at their disbelieving faces. "*Get going,*" he barked.

Cass wondered where that sort of junk could be found on such a clean, tidy ranch as she took Freedom around one more time. Earl propped poles atop cinder blocks that had been stacked inside the machine shed, a perfect height. Freedom worked up quite a lather by this time, and Cass admitted to herself that she, too, was tired. A nice tired. Legs tingled; insides of her thighs and knees felt raw and the helmet band was too tight, giving her a bit of a headache. She'd toughen up; she knew that. Now, walking slowly, reins loose on her horse's withers, a wave of pure contentment pressed into her chest.

Who would have thought? In my wildest fantasies, I wasn't even close to such...such...pure...oh...Freedom! Dismounting and handing the reins to Arthur, she thanked him and, still in a daze of happiness, went to join Bri and Sean. First she bent to drink the sparkling clear water that gushed invitingly from the fountain, allowing it to flow over her grimy face and neck before opening her dry, gritty mouth. Pure heaven! So cold it made her forehead ache, but so sweet it seemed unreal. *Makes city water taste like a mud-hole.*

"Okay, guys. Sean, you go get the flat wheelbarrow, I'll get empty grain bags from the feed room, and Cass, you change and have a bit of a breather, okay?" Bri was a super organizer.

"Great," chorused Sean and Cass.

"Oh, Cass. Almost forgot. A letter came for you. I put it on the kitchen table," and she strode off to the stable with Sean.

Letter? Who'd write me? Mom? Sal? Was something wrong? No – they'd use the phone. Cass's heart skipped a beat and a little thrill zapped around inside her.

Curiosity spurred her into a run. Excitement washed away her weariness as she bounced into the mud room, yanked off her boots with the wooden boot jack and hurried into the kitchen.

"Hi, Cassy! You looked good, girl!" This was Kayla's greeting. "I have a big glass of fresh squeezed orange juice ready for you." Reaching into the fridge, she handed the tall green glass to Cass as she passed by on her way to the table.

"Thanks, Kayla, I need this!" Leaning over the table she scanned the mail that was there, spotted a grubby envelope with her name and address on it, and felt her breath leave her. Who?

Setting down the glass, now sweating with teardrops of moisture trickling slowly down the sides, Cass picked up the envelope. She stared at it as though it might give her a hint of its contents. The postmark was unreadable; the stamp was a bit crooked. Someone with dirty hands had handled it. That didn't mean anything. Her mom must have given it to someone to mail for her. That was it. She tore it open. A torn page from a notebook; words written with a dull blue pencil. Her heart squeezed so tight it pained. She couldn't make her eyes focus. Tangy orange juice fumes made her stomach turn over.

Please, God, what's happening to me? Help me read this. Mom might need me.

"Cassy?" Kayla's voice came from far away. "Cass—what is it?"

"Just a letter," she murmured softly. And then she could see:

I KNOW WHERE YOU ARE

CHAPTER
FOURTEEN

Who knows where I am? It must be a joke. I don't know anyone that well anywhere for stuff like this. Sean? No, he wouldn't bother sending a note.

Head awhirl, trying to figure who wrote to her and why, Cass left the house on legs of rubber, to return to the ring. Earl's hands were full organizing where to dump chunks of branches, bricks, cinder blocks and old fence poles. He'd even dug up an old beat-up oil drum. Her heart leaped as a triple-toot car horn and a cloud of dust announced the arrival of two three-quarter-ton trucks into the stable area. Numb and distracted, Cass mounted Freedom and turned to the commotion.

Poppa! He'll know what to do…no, he might think I'm a wuss.

Absently, she fanned the dust cloud and gas fumes away from her face. A futile gesture. Chills encased her body. Emotions ceased to be.

Can't think of anyone who'd understand. Sal! No – she's too busy. I'll fix this myself – somehow.

"Crikey! They're early!" Sean dropped the end of a pole and charged toward the parking lot. "Whose red truck?"

Work stopped as all hands streamed out of the ring to see what was going on. Pat's truck was there, but who owned the shiny red one?

"Matt?" Bri stopped. Her jaw dropped. "No. It can't be."

Pat jumped out of his truck demanding, "What's going on here? What's all this trash doing in the training ring?"

"They're jumps, Dad. Cass and Freedom can really, really jump! Whose red truck?"

"Jumps? With that junk? She'll break her neck! Earl!" Pat never paused in his determined stride until he was close enough to kick the oil drum.

Cass still sat stiff and detached aboard an anxious Freedom, who was tossing his head in frustration.

"Thought the horse should get used to different stuff to jump over. The jumps in the horse show will be the real thing—different colors; got sides on them, sort of like chutes; then there are ones with water..." Earl was obviously enjoying himself

As Pat barked out orders, Freedom protested, shaking his head in frustration as Cass tried to hold him to a walk. No way. Prancing and snorting got them around the ring to stand by Earl.

"How come you know so much, old man?" Pat's eyebrows shot up, in doubt.

"I like to watch them jumping when we haven't any classes. Exciting, for sure."

Pat rubbed his chin for a moment, then out shot his hand—pointing straight at Cass. She didn't even blink.

"If you're going to have a chance at all, you'll need proper jumps. Now. This is what I want done: Bri—get a list of tack and riding gear that Cass will need, then take her to Denton or Ft. Worth and get it: Joshua, get a list of the official jumps that are used in these classes and get them here—fast! Earl, call the blacksmith and see if the horse needs special shoes. While you're at it call our supplier and get stall signs, feed pails, water pails and whatever else you can think of painted in our stable colors with Freedom's name on them."

"Dad! No! Our horses can't go English; it'll make us look like jerks!" Matt yelled in protest. The curt orders had reached the parking area where Matt leaned protectively against the door of the red truck.

"Spoken like a true man of vision—*tunnel* vision! Wake up, son! Get over here. There's a whole world out there that begs for someone—*any*one—to dare to be different. Look up the word "innovative" when you get to the house." Marching across the ring, he stopped beside Cass and Freedom. Over his shoulder he shouted, "I mean that, Matt." Giving Cass's leg a slap of excitement as she sat straight in the saddle he asked, "What do you want him to be entered under, Pine Image or Freedom?"

"Freedom!" Her stomach muscles clutched. She refused a name change and blurted, "He's been Freedom since forever for me!"

"What do you mean? No, he hasn't."

"Oh yes he has!"

Suddenly on the defensive, Cass became afraid the truth would burst this bubble of joy which surrounded her, but which now had become threatened. Shocked by her reaction toward the man she'd learned to love and trust, she lowered her head. Taking a steadying breath, Cass raised her head, looked Poppa straight in the eye, and swore to herself to fight whatever awaited her. She knew how to fight in the streets of New York, and was wise enough to know that she'd be using her common sense, brain and bull-headedness to fight for the right to stay here. This was home. Here she would stay, letter or no letter; name change or not.

"Right. Sal. The poster on your wall. I forgot about that." Poppa grinned, gave Freedom a friendly swat on the neck. "Freedom he is, and Freedom he'll always be!"

With a grateful smile, Cass turned her impatient mount toward the rest of the family. All talking at once, gesturing, laughing, arguing until Sean piped up in his strident battle cry.

"We work here, too!" With his face twisted in defiance, he whirled on his mother. "Mom! How come Matt's going to get paid and we aren't? We work even *harder* than him and now he's got a truck *and* money!"

Cass found herself surrounded by a family feud. *Now what am I supposed to do.*

" Mom, I've never thought of getting paid for what we do— it's what we're all about. You always make sure we have a few dollars when we head to town. Why should Matt get paid? I agree with Sean." Bri tossed her mane of glistening auburn hair in defiance.

Throwing her hands up in surrender, Momma began to laugh.

"It's not funny, Mom." Sean looked hurt. "Cass, what do you think? Don't you want to get paid for doing chores and training the horses?"

So that's the problem! I wish I'd stayed in the ring.

Now the focal point of the four Kileys, Cass's thought processes shut down completely. *I can't handle any more shit today.* Having no idea what was *really* going on, she automatically felt she should side with the kids. They sounded reasonable in their demands, but she was leaving in August, so who cares what she thinks. Nausea roiled in her throat as they stared at her expectantly. A familiar smell wafted into her system. Yes—fear does have a definite smell.

"Um, well I guess what's fair for one…" Shrugging, she let the comment hang. Sweat beaded on her forehead; her heart raced. *Have I just sealed my fate?*

"Okay, you guys. You've all had your say," Momma conceded. "This is part of America here…freedom of speech and all that…and I'm pleased to announce that your dad has it all figured out, so I'll let him do the negotiating." Still laughing she grabbed a couple of shopping bags from the back of the truck. "Come on, Bri—you, too, Sean—let's get this stuff up to the house."

Left alone with Matt, Cass's familiar fears continued their work. Her mouth filled with cotton balls and her heart beat an unsettling tattoo. *Please, God, not now. I'm over all that crap, right?* Freedom moved restlessly beneath her, sensing her rising panic.

"So—you're jumping over the moon now, are you?" No sarcasm, as she expected. "Incidentally, this is my truck, it's four years old, and I'm paying Dad out of my wages. He'll explain the deal. All of us will have time sheets to keep track of hours worked and the type of work done. And we'll get paid! Cool!" Hefting a huge bag of foal supplement onto his shoulder, he headed for the stables.

Cass remained mute. Shaking, she closed her eyes, resorting to an old method of getting herself back on track— deep, slow breathing. Yes. Think about the rolling hills around her; the foals kicking up their heels as the mares grazed peacefully.

Suddenly a large object hurtled against her chest and landed across the saddle.

Her piercing scream got Matt and his dad on the dead tear toward her.

"Cass! What's wrong?" Breathlessly Poppa reached up and pried her hands away from her face. Once that was done, Stray was able to stretch his head far enough to get in a couple of sloppy kisses as he panted and grinned in triumph.

"Stray! No!" Wiping her face with the tail of her over-sized tee shirt, she grinned in embarrassment at her two "saviors" who were bent over, howling with glee.

"I-I-I'm sorry. He scared me. I had my eyes shut."

This got Poppa going again while his son piped up, "Riding a horse with your eyes shut? Going to jump him that way, too?"

"Oh, shut up!" Tossing her head indignantly, she tapped her legs against her horse and walked him away from her source of humiliation. Steadying Stray against her, she marveled that Freedom hadn't flinched once during the chaos. In fact he seemed quite bored. What a horse. And what a dog. Where'd he learn to do that?

"Supper's on, Cass! Come and get it!" Bri's otherwise soft, low voice could carry a mile when she wanted it to.

"Be right there!" Cass put her brush on her dresser, stood, stopped and sat down again. The envelope. Curiosity made her pick it up for a closer inspection, and a lot more calmly than she had the first time. Still crumpled and dirty, Cass stared at it as if wishing it to give up its secret. She reached for the lamp and switched it on.

"Ah! *There* it is!" Holding the envelope close to the light bulb she could better see what was left of the postmark. Some of the date was visible, as was part of the circle. Within the circle, though, she couldn't tell if the position for the state showed a K or an X. New York or Texas. Hmmm. Head swimming with possibilities she couldn't pin down, Cass rose once again, laid the envelope down and made her way out of her bedroom. At the door she suddenly froze, her whole body felt like ice. *Tony!*

"Come on, Cass. Shake a leg." This time it was Poppa.

Like a wooden soldier, Cass moved down the stairs, along the hall, and to her place at the table. *I can't feel anything. I can't think. Stop it right now! It can't be Tony. He's gone. Sal said so. So did Mom.* These horrible flashbacks to when she used to feel this way all the time always unnerved Cass. She knew now that it would pass. But she had been so sure that she was now in control, that she'd never feel this way again. Now it was back.

"No! I won't let it!" The sound of her own voice shocked her. "Oops, sorry. I, um, was just thinking and that slipped out."

The family had stopped what they were doing and stared at her.

"Cass—what's wrong?" Momma laid down her fork, starting to get up.

"No, Mom, no. I'm sorry. Don't worry." She grinned sheepishly. "I'm just chasing away some old demons."

"Hey! I liked that—you called me Mom—finally! Mom and Dad—doesn't sound as temporary as Momma and Poppa. At least to me." Reaching over, she squeezed Cass's hand, smiling happily. "Now—about those demons—that's okay. Just keep chasing them and someday they'll leave for good." Mom blew her a kiss and everyone picked up where they left off. Calling their parents Mom and Dad was no big deal for the kids because that's who they were! But Cass knew she'd have a bit of a problem. She'd never called *anyone* Dad.

Dad's discussion now concerned the idea of starting an English Equitation Club at the ranch—the first in their entire area. Matt protested; the others were full of ideas and enthusiasm.

Cass still felt she was in the eye of a tornado, and wasn't tuned in to the discussion.

"We'll be the first in this neck of the woods to enter any of the English classes with a double registered horse at Ft. Worth. As for Denton, I think this is the first year they're going to have any jumping classes. At least, according to Earl."

"But, Pop—um—Dad, what if I make a mess of the jumping course?" Cass tuned in long enough to blurt out her fear.

"Hey, sweet girl, the name of the game is to do your best. Winning isn't why we show; not entirely. Yes, winning with our breeding stock is a feather in our cap because that's our business, but it's not the end of the world if we don't. There's always another show, another year, another horse, so we look forward to all the excitement, meeting old friends and competitors. We certainly don't get all warped out of shape if we don't win every time." He glanced at his kids. "Right, guys? Isn't that what I taught you? You gotta be a good loser, a humble winner, and an honorable competitor. And have yourselves a blast while doing your very best!"

All heads nodded as past shows were remembered and disasters discussed.

"I'm going to have brochures printed up and handed out at Denton, and put a nice ad in the papers all around here. That should stir up some interest—hopefully."

"Aren't you being a bit hasty, Pat? Maybe English isn't the way to go here. Maybe we should offer a Junior Western Club or something like that," offered Meg.

"Lordy, we have enough 4-H Clubs and pony clubs around here as it is." Wiping his mouth with the bright blue napkin, he stated firmly, "It will be English; all types and all ages. Period."

Reaching over to the sideboard he grabbed his pad of paper. Leafing through the first dozen sheets he finally found what he wanted and lay the pad down in front of him.

Cass was trying hard to concentrate on what was going on around her, but failed miserably. She could hardly catch her breath. Why so edgy? Nothing had changed. *What if I'm having a breakdown!* It sounded scary. She wasn't sure what a breakdown was, but had heard the word used at Haven House. Definitely bad news, and definitely what the Kileys didn't need to have in their home.

"...and Cass, here's your time sheet...Cass? You okay?" Pat was waving a sheet of paper at her. She forced her mind to focus.

"Yeah. Sure, Dad," and reached for the paper. It was all squared off with the days of the week at the top, a list of chores down the left side and a place for the total of hours each day at the bottom. There was a smaller square at the bottom right for the week's total.

"Any questions? I've listed everything including exercising

the horses, training one new horse and working with the foals; all stuff you're used to."

"What new horse? And, um, you don't have to pay me you know, Dad. I'll, um, be leaving and, y'know, you've already done so much for me, okay?" Squirming in her chair, Cass got the words out but wasn't sure her meaning was clear.

Pat leaned back in his chair and peered intently at Cass before he spoke.

"Cassy, you're here. You're not going anywhere and you work as hard as the others. I've got a new horse coming for you so that's two you have to train so you'll have two ready for the ring next show season. You hear me? *Next* show season!" Sitting forward, he planted his elbows on the table. "You'll get paid. End of discussion. Now, about the Denton show — Bri, have you figured out which classes you and Cass will enter? I know you'll both go Western *and* English, but what classes and when are they?"

Cass's ears were still ringing with the words 'next show season' and a single tear stung her eye. *Don't get excited. Don't expect too much. That way only leads to getting hurt, big time.* She could hear every beat of her heart. Dad wouldn't do that to her or to anyone. He always did what he said he would. How she'd get to stay till next year puzzled her as thoughts of school, her mother and Haven House flooded her mind. And now there's that letter. Dad must have a plan or he wouldn't have said anything — she felt the warmth of joy struggling to spread through her defense mechanisms. *Yes! It's okay — let go — be excited! I get to say Dad — I can't believe it! Dad!*

"Come on, Cass, let's take the dogs for a run through the woods, and we'll make plans," Bri suggested as the family left the table and started off in every direction.

Cass stood, pulled a tissue from her jeans pocket — and out flew the note. Swiftly, she snatched it from beneath her chair and crammed it back in her pocket. Breathing became difficult again; speech was impossible. Bri and Meg looked at her questioningly.

Cass couldn't say a word. Clutching her tummy, she whirled around and raced up the stairs to her room, shattered once again. Flinging herself onto the bed, she buried her head under the soft, downy pillows. Only then did she allow the fear to consume her, and with it came the shame of failure. One little letter had just undone all her promises to herself. Her fists hammered the pillows as deep sobs tore at her soul.

CHAPTER FIFTEEN

Mealtime at the Rocking K took on a whole new spirit these days. School was over for the year, exams had been agonized over, written and passed; school clothes were neatly delegated to the back of closets or into storage hampers; ranch clothes and show outfits now took prominent places in closets and on boot shelves. Conversations were lively from dawn till well after dusk, and all had to do with horses.

"Dad, I noticed Pak's colt is still trying to nurse. Shouldn't he be weaned by now? I want to show him at halter in Denton. His coloring is awesome!" Bri's concern competed with her bacon and eggs, but she was alert for her dad's reply.

"Yeah, Dad, more foals are late being weaned this year. What gives?" This observation was Matt's offering.

"Maybe it's just because of the hard winter. Remember the snow wouldn't quit?" This little whiff of wisdom came from Sean.

Pat grinned as he reached over and tousled the wavy red hair of his youngest. "From the mouths of babes!"

"I am not a 'babe'," came the retort, "But I know we were sure trucking out a lot of hay to the mares."

"You're partially right, Sean, but on top of that we had more mares due to foal a little later this year just for that reason. I'm not going to keep on with the anguish of worrying about the wee ones battling the snow and cold on top of everything else. Another four weeks or so doesn't make that much difference in the long run—not once you've got a reputation for good, solid stock like we do. We've been very fortunate that way."

Kayla appeared with a plate heaped with hot biscuits and a bowl of cut up fresh fruit. Hands shot out to claim possession of both favorites. Obviously bacon, eggs and toast didn't quite do it in this household.

"You've hardly eaten anything, Cass," observed Meg. "Feeling okay?"

"Yes, thanks. I'm okay." *Liar. I'm furious. At myself. Why do those awful feelings keep coming back to ruin everything? Okay, so maybe the note is from Tony. Big deal! What can he do to me here? Why is he threatening me now? Knock it off. Everyone is tiptoeing around me these days. Smarten up. Either talk to someone or forget about it.*

Stop screwing around!

"How's Brandy doing, Cass? Think she'll be ready for Western Pleasure?" Pat obviously wanted to bring her into the conversation.

Cass's eyes were glued to her plate, watching in fascination as her fork made patterns with egg yolk and bits of crisp bacon. The toast lay ignored. Looking up, her eyes didn't seek Pat's but aimed unseeing toward the riot of colored blossoms and bushes surrounding the patio. Finally she managed to speak.

"Brandy has her gaits down pat. She will do okay if I don't screw up." She sought out the congealing yolk once more.

"Do you like her? Is she comfortable to ride?" Pat persisted.

"Yes." The platter of hot biscuits that were offered her by Matt went unnoticed.

Silence.

Shrugs.

I can't do this. I can't! I feel like running, fast, in any direction, and never stopping, never having to think ever again. I want to cry like a baby and get rid of the pain inside me, but I can't. I've tried. There are no tears left. Someone help me—please! Sal! Her heart gave a weak flutter at this thought of hope, but soon languished again as she reasoned that Sal was too far away. The phone couldn't give her what she needed right now; she yearned for the right words accompanied by the warmth of nearness, of contact, of a hug. One lonely tear escaped. She kept her head down, forgot about her plate, which left her hands in tight fists at the edge of the table. *"Next year" Poppa-um-Dad had said. Words. Just words. He won't put up with me for much longer...and I love calling him 'Dad'. It sort of lets me love him for real...I wonder...*

Someone was speaking. Cass finally realized she was having her shoulders gently squeezed, and looked into the soft, gentle eyes of her new mom. *Please, God, help me make this last forever.* "Come with me Cass, I have something to show you."

Cass stood unsteadily, following Meg like a robot out onto the patio and down the path to the woods. One dazed step at a time. Sitting on the old familiar bench comforted her; breathing the blend of pungent pine cones, the carpet of fallen needles and, from somewhere unseen, the aroma of thick sweetness enveloped her. Maybe it came from the flower gardens. Whatever. Her physical pain receded allowing her mind the freedom for other thoughts.

Through all this, Meg had leaned back, head cradled on the high back of the bench and tanned legs stretched onto the path. Long lashed eyes were closed; the hint of a smile played at the corners of her silent lips.

"Mom?" Barely a whisper made its way to Meg.

"Mmmm...that sounded *so* nice...What is it, Cass?" Those glorious eyes bathed Cass with their honest caring.

"I don't know. I just don't know...I'm scared of so many things. I feel like I did way back, but then I knew for sure that I'd survive, that I'd figure something out. And I did. Now that feeling of *knowing* everything is going to be okay just isn't there anymore. I'm alone." Her long fingers pulled through her hair, slowly placing it behind her ears from where it immediately flowed back to partially cover her face. "I wonder why my guts have left me. I don't know how to fix it. I don't know how to handle stuff anymore. I hate this feeling of wanting to talk to someone, hoping it will make me feel better. That's selfish! *Everyone* has problems, so I should look after my own, right?" Realizing she was babbling, she bit her lip—hard. Glazed eyes sought the clean sky through the lacework of boughs, and the taste of blood was acrid.

Meg had hold of Cass's hand by this time and gave her a tug to slide over closer to her. "Well, my girl, when you decide to talk you sure do a fine job of it!" Smiling, she placed Cass's hand on her lap. "Now, let's see. Where should we start? Um...are you afraid of showing the horses?"

"No! That'll be fun!" For emphasis she waved her free arm in a circle.

"Okay. Now. Is it either Freedom or Brandy that worries you?" This question came more quickly, and got a quick answer.

"Definitely not!"

Meg shot the next question as if out of the barrel of a shotgun.

"Is it that letter you got in the mail?" Her eyes bored into Cass's, and held them there.

Cass let go of Meg's hand and placed both her hands on top of her bent head as if trying to hold it in place; as if trying to erase the question by not looking at Meg.

Meg waited, not moving, while Cass's tormented mind once again failed to come up with a coherent thought. Her heart was pounding and her body trembled. *Fool! Answer her! Get it out before it's too late and you lose everything you've learned to love! Talk! Stick your finger down your throat and puke the words out if you have to! Talk!*

Wrenching herself from the comfort of her brand-new mom and the old bench, Cass paced. And paced. Stopping in front of Meg at last, she tore the crumpled page from her pants pocket and dropped it onto Meg's lap as if it were a burning coal. Meg picked it up and carefully flattened it so she could read the words.

"'I know where you are'," she read aloud. Then repeated them slowly and softly.

"'I know where you are'. Is this supposed to be a threat, or what?" Meg was truly alarmed. "Someone obviously wants to let you know he or she knows where you are living now." Frowning, she stared at the creased note, finally asking, "What was the postmark?"

"I wish that was true, Mom, but I don't know anyone well enough for something like that."

"What was the postmark?" Meg repeated.

"That's just it—it wasn't all there. I could only make out something that was either a K or an X...New York or Texas maybe." Sitting again, Cass looked at the note.

"Capital letters, pressed hard into the paper means it could be a him," observed Cass.

"I agree, so who do you know in New York that would do this?" Meg's probing eyes demanded an intelligent and honest answer, and Cass knew it. Besides, the awful hammering in her chest had stopped; her thoughts were clear—just because she *talked* to Meg. Nothing was solved but she realized, without a doubt, that she was no longer alone. Confusion was replaced by clarity; fear was replaced by an unknown sensation deep in her soul. Was this trust? If so, it was taking her breath away with its all-consuming power.

"Well, Mom, I have the awful feeling that it's Tony, you know, the guy who always looked out for me all those years? The same guy who let those guys beat me up, and I don't know why, or what I did." Her head dropped as she whispered, "I just don't know—I'm afraid."

Meg put her arms around Cass's shoulders and hugged her to her chest. Cass slowly let the tension flow out of her body as she snuggled into Meg's warm arms. Silent tears poured from beneath closed lashes, and soaked Meg's sleeve.

"Leave it with me, baby," comforted Meg. "Dad and I will look out for you."

CHAPTER SIXTEEN

"It looks so *different!*" Cass had been past the fairgrounds a few times, and had seen the grandstand and huge fields, but hadn't really thought much about what went on there. Now it was full of brightly colored striped tents, vehicles of all descriptions, and now she could see the stable area, way at the back of the property.

In front of the grandstand, which was covered with red, white and blue bunting and American flags, was a large show ring, and beyond that a long line of big wooden stalls. Directly behind the stalls were pens that held cattle. Interesting. Maybe she should be looking at the program to see exactly what was going on here.

Oh, man! A rodeo! Bull riding! All she had noticed before were the barrel racing and calf roping. Barrel racing would be awesome because Bri was entered, but the calf roping part upset her. To her mind, that was cruel. The bulls—well—that was a different matter. They were big enough to fend for themselves, and she could hardly wait to watch. Scanning through the pages, she could see that someone in the family would be showing every day of the week-long show. At first it was mostly halter classes for the foals, weanlings and breeding stock. It seemed that all the jumping events were either late afternoon or early evening, with the Pleasure, Equitation and Showmanship, both Western and English, being held in the afternoons. Rodeo events were in the evenings, as they were the crowd pleasers.

Putting the program in her backpack, Cass thought about how much she had to learn. Then, like a bolt out of the blue, it dawned on her how much she had *already* learned in a few short months. Smiling to herself at the warm shimmer of inner pride, she promised herself that she was going to be the best that she could be. No more wallowing in the past. It was gone and she couldn't change it. But she *could* move on, move past it. This, she was convinced, could happen by watching everything that goes on around her, and trying to be as helpful as possible. Bits and pieces of her talk with Meg kept popping into her mind now and then, always leaving her feeling a bit stronger and a lot more determined not to allow herself to slide into those scary downers.

"You're awfully quiet all of a sudden," observed Matt as he slowly steered his truck through gates, between stables, stopped for the wandering public and ended up beside the last stable, where the Rocking K had stall space.

"Just thinking," mused Cass. "So much has happened, and changed. The way I look at things now is so much clearer, y'know, sort of different than before."

"Before what?"

"Everything!" She caught his crooked grin. "It's not funny! It's weird." Twisting in her seat she put her hand on his arm, shook it gently and stated, "Sure, I was a basket case when I first got here, but—think about it—ever since I got better there have been such awesome things happening to me, y'know?"

Matt lifted his left hand from the steering wheel and squeezed her hand on his arm. "Yeah, Cassy. I know."

Sighing, he continued, "And not only to you, either. I understand how you got messed up, for sure, but I can't *believe* the things I've done, didn't do, said—aw, jeez—what a prize jerk I've been. A spoiled brat. And if you asked me what smartened me up, I couldn't tell you."

"Well, getting your own truck didn't hurt." A bit of humorous sarcasm crept into Cass's voice.

"No! I was starting to sort things out before that trip to Ft. Worth." Angry that he was defending himself, he blurted "You were too blinded by your own freak show to notice anybody else!"

"That's not fair!" Lifting her hand from his arm, she punched his upper arm, making him yell. She had been a bit sneaky, and made her middle knuckle stick out farther than the rest, ensuring it would hurt him worse.

"Jeez, Cassy! You fight dirty!" His contagious belly laugh filled the cab, and they rolled to a stop beside Pat's rig.

Such a difference. When did it happen? Why did it happen? Was she finally trusting, allowing herself to feel love? No! She couldn't fall in love with Matt! He was like a brother. *Well...not really...*

"Quit horsing around, you two, and get that thing unloaded. Earl! Leave my truck for the boys to unload; you stay close to the horses. I don't want any accidents." And he was gone.

"Father has spoken! We'd better move it!" Bri joined Matt and Cass, and they began the tedious task of shunting gear from trucks to stable. Once that was done, the *real* work started. Putting up shining brass racks for bridles, halters, saddles, hangers for a wall draped with previously won championship ribbons. *Ohmigod! This is too much! Good smells; bad smells; hammers banging in nails; curses when hammer hit thumb...*Giggling, Cass realized they were all staring at her, so she grabbed a bridle to hang on a brass rack. Back to work. Furniture had to be placed. A table, comfortable chairs that pulled out to make beds for Earl and Josh, a big brass mirror, a cabinet that held everything with which to make fast food, a microwave and a huge coffee maker completed their tack room. Outside, the tack room and box stalls would be adorned with heavy cotton burgundy and gold drapes—their stable colors. Every horse and foal had its name on a gleaming plaque that hung on its stall door, and every horse had its name on a feed pail, water pail, and fly sheet. Each horse wore the colorful cover to protect it from bothersome gnats, flies and dust.

The beehive of activity nearly finished Cass, but she kept up with the rest of them, following orders, watching others and copying them, and all the time marveling at what went on behind the scenes at a horse show. She never, ever gave this sort of thing a thought. Neither did the family, because none of it was mentioned. Having done this so often, year after year, she figured it was just ho-hum stuff to the Kileys.

Cass was totally overwhelmed. She couldn't remember ever being so excited. She kept checking on Freedom and Brandy, discovering that this little diversion settled her down. Although Brandy kept her head poked out of her stall, watching every bit of action, Freedom had his head lowered, pointed at the back corner of his stall, snoring gently. This guy didn't have a nerve in his body.

Aware that the Kileys were secretly keeping an eye on her, worrying about the upset that had prompted the chat with Meg, Cass was surprisingly upbeat. What was it Earl had said to her one day—*a burden shared is a burden halved*—or something like that. That's how Cass felt. Lighter—inside and out.

"Great job, you guys!" Pat's voice boomed through the stable. "Take turns on guard duty and go get your supper. Do you all have your meal tickets?" Heads nodded and a few of the stable-hands strolled through the stable toward the big dining tent over near the grandstand. The food was really good. Nothing fancy, but lots of it. None of the fast food type of thing; just good down-home cooking.

Meg and Bri appeared just then and Cass realized she hadn't seen them for ages.

"Where did you go? You missed all the fun. Look what we did." Cass's arm swept the scene in their stable. "Ta-da! Beautiful, right?"

"It sure is! And it's finished already — well done!" Meg walked over to check on her favorite foal, which she had named Blarney. His registered name was a mile long, but Blarney was his stable name. "They traveled well for little fellas," she commented. "Did the boys have any trouble with them?"

"No, not at all. Archie and Juan stayed in the trailer with them, and they said they were real troopers." Cass's tummy growled. Meg heard it.

"I have a brilliant idea — let's go eat!" Laughing, the three of them left but, instead of going to the tent, Meg went over to the truck. "Come on, get in. I'm starved."

"Where are the guys?" Cass looked around for Sean and the others.

"They have to pick up something in town and plan to eat there, explained Meg. "We, on the other hand, are going to the best chicken fried steak joint in Texas, barring Kayla's, of course!"

Wagon wheel lighting fixtures, wagon wheels topped with glass for tables, all sizes, shapes and colors of wagon wheels covering the barn board walls, and for color there were splashes of paint that remotely resembled trees and shrubs standing out boldly between the wheels.

"I'd never guess why this place is called The Wagon Wheel," Cass drawled.

"Yeah, but it's the best food going and they're fast," defended Bri. "I'm going to get the special — it comes with a drink and dessert."

"Me, too." Meg raised her brows questioningly at Cass. "Okay, me too," she agreed, "What's the special?"

"Chicken fried steak! We already told you!" Bri shook her head in disgust.

"Come on, girls, no bickering. We're hungry and snarly, so until the food comes let's make sure we know what we're doing tomorrow." Putting the show program on her bright red plastic place mat, Meg took a pen from her bag and opened up to the saddle horse section. "Halter classes in the morning, as usual; Equitation, Pleasure and Horsemanship till mid-afternoon, then Barrel Racing. Let me see — yes, there's Barrel Racing every day, same time, but Hunter and Jumper classes go through supper until around 7:30." She slapped the program shut. "Then the fun starts! My favorite — Bull Riding!"

"Mother!" Bri never could understand that such a wild streak could exist in this otherwise down-to-earth and worldly-wise parent.

"What?" demanded Meg.

"Oh, never mind."

Cass tried not to show her delight in this exchange, and was glad when their dinners appeared. The conversation turned to issues like outfits for each event, tack for all the horses, then on to harmless gossip. Earl and Joshua were in charge of caring for the horses, so they were well looked after. Meg double-checked everything. She hated surprises.

"SURPRISE!"

Matt, Sean and their dad sneaked in with a big birthday cake, lighted candles and all. Patrons and staff all sang a rousing, off-key version of "Happy Birthday" to Bri.

Stunned, Bri stammered, "But it's not until next week."

"We know, but we wanted you to show Blarney in the weanling class for his new owner." Her dad grinned mischievously.

A BRANCH FOR CASS

"Who?" Bri was totally confused.

"YOU!" they yelled in unison. "HAPPY SIXTEENTH!"

Insides jiggling like jelly, heart pounding and palms so damp she kept rubbing them down her riding pants, Cass made a huge effort to appear calm—like an old pro. She knew no one was fooled. Approaching Freedom for about the fifth time to check him over, to make sure there was nothing wrong with him, made her feel better.

"Look, Earl. His head is hanging. His back foot is resting on its toe. He doesn't feel well!" Total alarm swarmed around her like an impenetrable aura that no one could dispel—yet.

"Look here, Cass, for the umpteenth time I'm telling you your horse is just fine. He's resting." Shaking his head, he took Cass gently by the arm and led her over to Meg. "Here, Missus. She's all yours. I can't get through to her."

Immediately Cass turned to Meg, breathlessly repeating her fears for her horse.

"Earl's right, Cassy. Freedom has the ability to sleep anywhere, anytime, and that's a big plus. When he's asked to perform, he'll become a different horse—you wait and see." Meg dusted off the black velvet safety helmet, tucked wayward strands of blonde hair back into the tight little bun at the back of Cass's neck, and took a couple of swipes at her black riding jacket. Satisfied, she once again turned to watch the events going on in the ring, which was the wind-up of the Junior Equitation (Western, of course). It looked like Sean was going to be in the ribbons. He captured a big, long, satiny pink fifth with his foal in the morning, which had him over the moon, so to get placed in this would send him into orbit.

Matt won with his yearling in the line class, and nailed another first in the Novice Reining—no small feat! Joshua's stallion was Overall Champion, while Bri swept the Barrel Racing, Western Equitation, Western Pleasure, and was now waiting with Cass to compete in Hunter over Fences. She was as excited as Cass, but not the least bit nervous. This was old hat to her, showing horses, but the rush she got before each class showed in her flushed cheeks and wildly sparkling eyes. Cass hoped that some of Bri's calm-under-fire would rub off on her, but the butterflies in her tummy and her third race for the washroom told her that she had a long way to go.

Her eyes swept the crowded grandstand, so colorful and noisy, and then took in an even bigger crowd jammed up around the ring itself, and flowing toward the food and drink tents. In the near distance was the fair itself with all the music, shrieks and laughter that usually accompanies joyful thrills.

I can't believe all this. I don't know what I feel; excited, for sure; scared, definitely; but worried? No. Not worried. I have to admit this is totally beyond...beyond...

"What's with the grin?" A poke in the ribs broke her reverie as Matt joined her.

"Just happy, I guess," and she gave him a gentle punch on the chest. "How about those wins earlier today? That's great, Matt. You've had a terrific week."

"Thanks. It's been a good one for me. Bri, too." His big blue eyes squinted in the sun as he watched Sean put old Zippola through a figure of eight at the lope. "That kid's a natural. He'll go far if he sticks with it." Turning back to Cass he reminded her of their early chats that always ended up with bitter words. "It was all my doing, Cass. I admit not once did I think about the horror you'd just escaped from. It was all me, me, me! Dad says kids our age go through feelings they don't understand, that it's sort of a rite of passage. All I know is that I was so mixed up I didn't know what I felt. It all came out as anger even when I wanted so badly to be happy, to laugh and, yes, to even hug *you*, like this." With a whoop, Matt threw his arms around Cass and lifted her off her feet. Her scream had heads turning in gleeful anticipation of a fight.

"Smarten up, you two. You'll upset the horses!" Meg was not amused, but everyone else was laughing. With his arms still snugly wrapped around her, Cass realized warmth and calm she'd never had before. Her heart did a few loops, too. *This is crazy! Why him? Why now? Don't be stupid – he's just goofing around. Don't forget those names he used to call you. Don't forget his moods.* Laughing, Cass stepped away from Matt, went over to Freedom, and mounted.

"Good luck." Matt gave her boot a slap as he walked by. *Don't forget – he's changed – and for sure, don't forget how much you've changed.* Watching his tall figure disappear in the crowd, she sighed and hoped he'd be at the ring to watch. Annoyed that she felt stronger, taller, bigger than life right at this moment, she knew she didn't have time to deal with it. She had a job to do.

"Don't look so worried. Just take him in and aim him. He'll do the rest."

"Yeah, right, Bri. Thank goodness the course isn't complicated, and there's no water jump."

"Just have fun out there. You did fine in the Pleasure and Equitation, so this is no big deal. This is what you do best."

"Sure, we placed – barely – but it didn't feel like a competition to me. It was just like all of us working in the ring together at home." Reaching down, she stroked Freedom's neck. He was more alert now, seeming to know that soon he'd be working. "This is different. All alone in front of all these people!" She pretended to shiver.

"There's got to be a first time for everything, so grit your teeth and get it over with. Now, come on, they've got the jumps in place. I'll lead you to the gate." Bri was excited but hid it well. Cass knew that those rosy cheeks were pure glee, and all because of her. *What if I let her down? Or let the whole Rocking K down! This is the first horse to jump from their ranch. God, I wish I hadn't thought of that.* Now her heart really did turn over, and as luck would have it, the loudspeaker called her number. *I go first! Crap!*

"Hey, great! You get to go first." Bri ran beside her to the gate then swatted her butt on the way by. "Luck, Cassy!"

"Let 'er rip, Cassy!" A quick glance showed her that the entire group from the ranch had crowded up to the rail to root for her, and then they were erased from her mind as she circled once and headed Freedom for the first jump. Count the strides, feel his mouth, squeeze him over, look at the next jump, count the strides, feel his mouth, gather him for the triple bar, look at the next jump. The gleaming coat of the horse caught the sunlight and every muscle and ripple showed as he propelled himself gracefully over jumps, across the ring to approach another, then another. Cass felt each powerful thrust of Freedom's hindquarters, each eager turn into another obstacle, and it energized her. She flew, soared, horse and rider—a fused unit of drive and energy.

"Yessss! Clean round!" Sean was first to reach her when she trotted out of the ring, almost getting himself run over by the next horse in.

I did it! I don't remember it, but I did it. Clean. This is fun. Look at the time...wow!

Pat took Freedom's reins and ran with him, off to one side away from the crowd, with the whole clan close behind.

"How do you feel?"

"Were you scared?"

"You looked like an old pro out there."

"Get down so I can towel him off and check his feet." This order came from Earl. Joshua rubbed the horse's face. Freedom was enjoying this royal treatment immensely, making little moaning noises in his throat, snorting softly, making sure he kept his head low enough so Joshua could have a good go at him.

Cass laughed as she unbuttoned her jacket, trying for some cool air where there was nothing but heat and dust.

" I can't believe it—it went so fast—I didn't see a thing but the jumps—all those people just weren't there, and I was so scared they'd spook me or the horse—and he just took everything in stride, just like at home—and ..." Meg's hand clamped over her mouth.

"Hold on there, tiger, you'll wear yourself out."
The crowd roared as the horse now in the ring made his round. Matt was standing on tiptoe as an alarmed groan smothered the sound of horse, rider and jump crashing to the ground. "It's Mandy Collins," announced Matt. He pushed forward for a better look. A round of applause indicated that horse and rider were back on their feet and on their way out of the ring.

Finally Earl gave the signal, and once again Cass mounted Freedom as all the contestants gathered at the gate. While they stood there, watching the last competitor, a jet-black gelding, fly over the triple bar. He tipped the middle rail with his hind hoof. Cass felt sorry for the rider. He would have had a clean round. But she didn't have much time to think, because the loudspeaker called for their attention.

"Will the following numbers return to the center of the ring, please?" The booming voice listed off numbers, and Cass watched as those entries walked proudly in to get their ribbons. She turned, smiled at Bri and started to say something when Earl chirped at Freedom and walked him to the gate, giving him a happy slap on the rump as he walked on into the ring, following the other two horses. Cass did absolutely nothing.

W-wha — ? Did we win something? This is different. I should be paying attention. What happens now? Settle down and quit behaving like a greenhorn. Just follow those guys and do what they do. Look like you do this every day. Where did we place?

As if in answer to her silent question the ringmaster beckoned, indicating where she should line up. She did, not looking left or right. The judge and ringmaster soon stood at Freedom's head, and clipped a flowing white ribbon onto the side of his headband. The horse tossed his head to make sure everyone saw his prize, and Cass smiled, bowed her head a bit in respect, whispering a thank you.

Ohmygod – a third! We got a third!

This time she couldn't pretend this was 'old hat'. As the five horses cantered briskly around the ring, heading for the gate, Cass thought her face would crack. She couldn't stop smiling – even laughing – with pure joy. This was awesome! How come they got a ribbon? Jeez Louise! At this point she was swarmed by whooping Kileys and their overjoyed ranch hands, seeing the fruits of their labor rewarded.

"Atta girl! Well done!" Pat slung his arm behind her on the saddle while Meg grabbed onto and held her hand. Sean beat on her boot; Bri held onto her dignity, giving her a huge smile and a thumbs up.

Tears of utter joy and relief streamed down Cass's grinning face, but when she turned to answer something Matt said, her face froze. Her heart stopped. She must have gasped or blurted a denial because Matt reached up and took hold of her arm.

"Cassy, what's wrong?" He shook her arm to get her to look at him. She didn't. "Come on, Cass!"

"No…no…no…" she murmured. Blinking rapidly, she refocused her eyes, chanced another, closer look, this time meeting his eyes. Those huge, brown trusting eyes…

"He – him – Tony." Pointing, moaning softly, "He's the one…he let them beat me up…why, Matt…why?"

CHAPTER
SEVENTEEN

Now a working girl, in spite of her torn and shredded dreams, Cass never stopped. Pat told her to cool it—"Rome wasn't built in a day." Yeah, okay, but escaping the confusion roiling around in her mind and in her soul was a whole lot easier when she worked herself into a lather. This was easy, during the unbelievably hot Texas summer. Getting used to the dry scorching heat was a definite trial for Cass. Having spent all her life at the mercy of the humid, suffocating summers and sub-zero biting winds in New York City, her system revolted. Simply breathing was a chore.

Tony's here! No doubt about it now. I can't run — I owe too much to Mom and Dad. Besides, I don't think I'd want to live without them. Bending over to pick up a mare's hoof to check it, she was broadsided by Stray, tongue lolling, grinning with pure joy. Jesse and Sam were on a hunting trip, heads down, tails wagging and not a single sign of their prey in sight. *Great imaginations, those dogs have.*

Leaving the hoof on the ground Cass turned to Stray. "That's a no-no, Stray! You could've spooked Molly and hurt me." While this feeble excuse for discipline was being meted out, Cass was rubbing the soft black ears lovingly. Straightening up, she put her hands on her lower back and stretched to her full height. Her eyes scanned the mares and foals, looking for anything out of the ordinary. All was well in spite of the disturbance created by Jesse and Sam darting around and beneath the patient mares. A few foals tried to join in but soon got bored and decided to frolic and kick up their heels off by themselves. Cass didn't blame them; there was a soft, warm wind bathing the ranch during this hour before supper, bringing with it all the serene sounds that nature provided. A quiet time. A peaceful time. Pristine puffs of clouds dotted the blue, blue sky.

If only this could go on forever – a person could heal if the world would stay out of the way.

Picking Molly's hoof up and placing it between her knees, Cass dug around the frog and sole, checking for cracks, pebbles wedged in tender places and possible cracks at the hairline of the hoof. Cass cracked up when she first heard that the v-shaped pad in the hoof was called a frog, of all things. Why frog? Then there was a discussion that had something to do with the Italian word for fork—*forchetta*, or something—which the pad was supposed to look like. Personally Cass thought it looked more like an arrowhead. Sounded more reasonable to her than frog did.

The past couple of hours spent checking out the mares had settled her down enough that she was humming to herself. Before long, she heard the strident strains of the Irish Pipes and Drums being flung across the skies of the ranch. Turning, Cass grinned, loving every beat of it. Knowing the beloved Irish music would be broadcast for at least fifteen minutes, Cass slowly strolled among the sleek, placid herd of brood mares, making her way home. She reached the gate by the woods as 'Danny Boy' began its sad refrain, and had to admit that she was beginning to like this strange music.

Approaching the patio, she heard the Kiley clan loudly and lovingly singing their hearts out.

"You guys are in tune for a change." Cass grinned, walked over to them and joined in. She thought this was a great way to announce the end of the work day, and the call to supper. Sure beat yelling all over the place till everyone was rounded up.

Cass eagerly attacked the tender roast beef and gravy which, with vegetables done to perfection, was her favorite meal. She tried valiantly to take in the table conversation, but for a while was too busy eating, convinced she was a borderline starvation victim. Working all day in the great outdoors did wonders for the appetite.

The discussions were all about Ft. Worth and the horses they were planning to take. Bri was working on two horses for jumping and her usual two for Western classes; Sean had his hands full with his weanling and Dillon, a five-year-old chestnut Paint gelding his father thought he was ready for, and was doing well with; Matt had two reining stallions and a mare he was working with for cutting.

Cass joined in, loud and clear, when it came to *her* horses. She had Freedom and Brandy for jumping and hunter classes, as well as English Pleasure and Equitation. A third horse, a double-registered mare named Tralee, was almost ready for the show ring and it was with her that Cass spent most of her time. Freedom and Brandy had regular workouts in order to keep fit, and to keep their timing sharp, but Tralee was in full training mode in hopes of taking her to Ft.Worth. Cass was determined to meet the challenge, and produce a half decent Green Hunter and Pleasure competitor with Tralee. So far all was going well.

Other than that, the meal continued without her input because, for some reason, her power of concentration was being badly undermined by thoughts of Tony: Why he was here? Why had he sent the note? Was he being sought by the police or the Marauders? On and on the unanswerable questions went, and that was the problem. She was no longer haunted by blind fear, nor did she feel as frightened about doing something wrong and being hauled back to Haven House. An inner strength had developed somewhere along the way. It probably was the result of the Kileys and their faith in her. Then again, maybe it was because she was learning, doing and succeeding at a whole new way of life in which she now felt comfortable. She was no longer afraid of failure, because she had discovered that it wasn't the end of the world if she screwed up; she just tried again until she got whatever it was right. Only one thing snagged at the back of her brain: August. That's when school started in Texas. Here it was almost July and no mention of any of it. Cass knew she sure wasn't going to ask about it! To her that was tempting fate.

Coffee and dessert were enjoyed on the patio—a tradition in good weather. The gardens were in show-shape, according to Pat. It was an atmosphere that Cass thought she'd never take for granted, because she had never known of the existence of such beauty. A perpetual explosion of vivid colors and enchanting whiffs of ever-changing perfumes overwhelmed her. The combination served as a panacea for all that bothered her. Glancing at Matt who was standing to one side chatting with his father, she remembered how she felt when his arms enfolded her. An unsettling memory for the simple reason that, if it should happen again, she didn't know how to handle it. Did she want him to kiss her? No, she didn't think so. That would be uncomfortable. Cass felt the closeness that was growing, for sure. Whatever it was, it felt solid and good, but not what she thought of as a romantic closeness. At least, she didn't think so, but...

"HAPPY BIRTHDAY TO YOU, HAPPY BIRTHDAY TO YOU, HAPPY BIRTHDAY DEAR CASSY, HAPPY BIRTHDAY TO YOU!"

Cass was on her feet, stunned beyond words, and stood

open-mouthed, staring at the family as they sang and Kayla carried a huge cake to the glass table.

"Blow out the candles! Make a wish!" Sean dragged her across to the table as everyone grabbed her for a hug. Wild laughter was almost drowned out by Matt's huge speakers that were aimed through the patio doors, thundering out the latest hit parade songs.

Confusion. Total and absolute confusion. Her heart hammered; she shook like a leaf; she didn't know whether to laugh or cry, so she did both—her birthday! She hadn't given it a thought. Birthdays had always been just another day, except she got to be a year older. This—this had her floored. A huge pink 16 made of rich icing stood an inch high in the center of a work of art. Such a beautiful cake!

"Hurry up! The candles are dripping!" Sean again, so she took a big breath and blew them all out. Everyone applauded as if she'd done something fantastic, then Kayla brought a long silver knife for Cass to cut the first slice. So she did, and turned to Meg.

"Oh, Mom! Thank you so much." Holding out her arms she stepped close to Meg and hugged her with a depth of emotion she never knew she had.

"You're so very welcome, Cassy. We had a problem keeping it a secret with Sean's big mouth—but we did it! What fun!" Tilting her head back, she asked, "Did you make a wish?"

"What for? A wish? I've already got everything in my wildest dreams!"

"You're supposed to make a wish when you blow out your birthday candles, and when you make the first cut into the cake."

"Oh. Well, maybe next time I'll do that. I've never heard of such a thing." Cass reached for her glass of lemonade.

"SURPRISE!" And over went the lemonade, smashing the glass onto the deck.

"Oh, my God!" she shrieked, hands over her ears.

"Here. Open it!" Sean handed her a gaily wrapped box with pink ribbons curling all over the place.

"But the glass—it's broken. Mom, I'm so sorry."

"Forget it. Open it—*now.*" Sean began to foam at the mouth.

"What is this? A present?" Cass turned the box over, then over again. "It's so pretty!"

"Open it! Now!" Sean hopped around in his excitement.

"Okay. Okay." Off came the ribbons, and she tried to get the paper off without tearing it. This was too much for Sean. He reached over and clawed the paper, tearing it completely off the box.

"There. Open it!"

Lifting the lid, Cass found something wrapped in pink tissue paper, and when she had that torn off she was holding a pink nylon foal halter. She just stared at it. A feeling of expectancy welled within her, but she didn't know why. Clutching it to her chest she leaned over and kissed Sean on the cheek.

"Thanks, Sean. It's beautiful. I can put this on my wall beside the ribbons I won." Smiling broadly she held out the little halter for all to see, just as proud as she could be.

"Let's see if it fits," Matt called out.

He stood at the edge of the patio with Molly's little filly, who stared wide-eyed at all the glitter and bright lights. In the background, Cass could see Earl holding Molly, ensuring that the foal would find a refuge if she got scared. But she wasn't scared at all—she was downright nosey, and slowly put one tiny hoof ahead of the other until she reached Cass.

"Hi, little girl. You coming to my party?" Cass crooned softly while stroking the jet black neck. The filly's white areas were startling against the black, and were in perfect areas of her body. Both forelegs were white, coming to an inverted V on her chest; her hind legs were white up to her hocks; her tail — what there was of it — was mostly white at this point, but when she matured that could change. But Cass had loved the dear little face of this youngest member of the Rocking K since she first laid eyes on her. A perfect white diamond on her forehead joined a perfect pink diamond on the tip of her soft, tiny nose by an absolutely straight, narrow line of white. Her markings were stunning as far as Cass was concerned, and she'd fantasize about her in the show ring, and how she'd stand out like a jewel among the other horses. Jazz — her very private name for this adorable and gentle little filly. *I wish you and I could always be like this — close — loving...*Jazz's high-pitched version of a whinny broke everyone up, and certainly jolted Cass's daydream. *Some day! Some day I'll be able to own a horse, maybe not as grand as Jazz, but maybe I could love it almost as much as I do her and Freedom. I'm happy even to have them on loan for the summer — just look at all that's happened — through good and bad, everyone here pulls together. Guess I've discovered how families are supposed to be, and that's a plus.*

Pat and Meg joined Bri and Sean as they gathered near the edge of the patio. Molly nickered softly to her baby, who ignored her completely.

"Happy Birthday, Cassy. This baby girl is yours. All yours. You'll have to come up with a name we can register, and a stable name. Any foals she has in the future will be yours." Pat's smile was so gentle. So really, really loving. Cass couldn't speak. She swallowed several times, blinked back tears but was scared to say anything, because the only thing in her mind was that she'd have to leave her filly when she left in August. She was so horribly torn between the unbelievable joy of the moment, and the pending heartbreak, that words just wouldn't come. Her heart ached with soaring joy — and with the certainty of loss.

"That's okay, my girl. You've been walloped with surprises this evening. We'll give it time to sink in, okay?" Pat put an arm around her and gave her a gentle squeeze. "But first, Mom and I have something to ask you." He walked Cass over to the door and then in to the dining area where several papers lay on the table.

"Have a seat, Cass. You too, Meg." Pat sat and gathered the papers closer to him, then reached over to take Cass's hand. Meg grasped her other one in both of hers.

" We—all us Kileys—were wondering if you'd like to become a member of our family. Our daughter." His blue, blue eyes searched her face as if willing her to agree, half afraid she wouldn't.

Cass's lips were parted, her eyes glued to the papers on the table, but she remained silent. *How can this be happening? What does it mean? Dreams just don't come true! What about my Mom and school? Won't there be trouble?*

"You're worried about something, Cassy," Meg stated tenderly. "Let's hear it."

Looking Meg in the eye for a long, long moment, then turning to Pat, Cass finally whispered, "What does this mean? What about—everything—y'know—my Mom—Haven House—stuff like that. School, too." Having stammered out her fears, she searched their faces, one then the other, wanting the answers to make everything all right.

Pushing the papers in front of Cass, Pat explained that her mother signed the consent form to allow the adoption of her daughter by the Kileys. This in no way meant she wasn't still her mother who loved her very much; it meant she was giving Cass a chance at life that she never could. They would always be able to phone, write, even see each other, but Cass would legally be a Kiley in every way. She had already been registered in the same school as Matt, Bri and Sean.

"Is that what you want, Cassy? If not, we understand, but already we feel as if you are ours and always have been."

Unable to grasp the full meaning of all this, her *heart* understood, and that was all that mattered. She could only nod and sob, hearing the high-pitched whinny of her little filly in her new pink halter, waiting for her outside with her brothers and sister.

Blinking rapidly Cass cleared away the tears enough to see the official seal beside her name on the adoption papers.

Cassandra Kiley.

"Cassandra Kiley," she whispered in awe, a slow smile fighting its way through the tears. "But I'll need a middle name," and laughter broke the emotional strain of the last few moments.

"Come on, daughter. We've got an announcement to make!"

Arms entwined, the three of them stepped out onto the patio where a huge cheer went up. Even the cowhands were there with their wives and kids. They all knew!

"I feel a party coming on!" shouted Pat over the uproar. "Music, Matt, if you please!"

CHAPTER EIGHTEEN

It's true! I'm a Kiley. They aren't going to send me back to New York! They can't now…can they? No, you jerk — stop looking for trouble.

"Cassandra Kiley. Cass Kiley. Cassy Kiley. *Ewww…*definitely not." She hoped no one could hear her. The full name sounded best to her, but she knew "Cass" would stick. She wished it was "Sandra" — it sounded best of all. Middle names escaped her. All she could think of were Ann, Marie, Lee, Elaine — blah! None of them clicked with her first name. Never mind — not important. But she had to get her little filly registered so she should concentrate on her. Dad would have to help, because she wanted to include the proper bloodlines. Cass had been calling her Jazz, or Jazzy, since she was born for no particular reason. Perhaps it was her startling color. So, Jazz it will stay.

Moving on to another mare, Cass picked up her front hoof and picked away at it, then realized she wasn't concentrating. Flashes of big brown eyes in an Italian face kept flooding her mind, even though she fought against it. Tony. The image always made her feel nervous and upset. But there was no reason for it. Absolutely none. So he was here in Texas, at the Denton show. He couldn't hurt her now, that's for sure. This thought never failed to make her feel able to handle anything that was thrown at her. Maybe it was just that hollow, hurting sense of betrayal that she couldn't erase from her mind, or her heart. Her Tony. Her hero. How could he?

"Why are you just standing there? Are you sick?" Sean. Where had he come from? She hoped she hadn't been thinking out loud.

"Just giving my back a rest." Quick thinking, girl.

"You sound like Mom and you're not even old yet."

"Right. I hoped someone would come along to finish up with Bonny so I could head home for supper."

Sean stared at her for a moment, grabbed the hoof pick from her hand and with quick motions cleaned and checked the rest of Bonny's hooves. Without a word he handed back the pick and turned for home.

"Hey, wait up. Thanks, Sean." Catching up to him, Cass asked, "Why did you come out here?"

"Oh. Forgot. Everyone's packing for Ft. Worth and Mom wants to be sure you've got everything done right. The stuff's being loaded tonight." Sounding important and strutting like a rooster, he added, "My work's already done."

"Oh." Cass bit the inside of her cheek to keep from laughing. "Guess I'd better get a move on then."

"Supper first."

Knowing she'd been told, but good, Cass kept on walking to get to the house before he said anything else to endanger her self-control. Her giggle-meter was at the exploding point.

It had finally arrived — Travel Day — and Cass rolled up her sleeves to pitch in. Leg protectors were wrapped around the legs of every horse, even though the trailers were thickly padded over every inch of the interior. Two CM 6-horse trailers meant twelve horses plus all their gear. Handlers traveled right in the stalls with the young stock to keep them calm during this, their first road trip.

The boys rode with Pat in his crew-cab while the girls joined Meg in the RV. With them were all the clothes, first aid kits, medications for horses and humans, plus many other necessary odds and ends. The RV would be used for changing into their show gear, getting cleaned up and grabbing a few hours sleep. The family had reservations at the Worthington, which was downtown, so they could escape the crush and turmoil of the fairgrounds once in a while.

Beautiful, rolling green countryside flashed past as they headed down the highway with Pat in the lead. The two horse rigs followed behind him, and Meg's RV brought up the rear. She could keep an eye on everything ahead of her, and had her cell phone to give Pat a heads-up in case of problems.

Cass and Bri chattered like magpies about who they thought would be at this show, how their horses would stack up against the competition; they wished they had done this or that differently, and even wondered if Dad would take some horses to the new World's in Arizona this year. Like Dad said, they were well-known for their horses, so maybe they'd stick closer to home. Arizona was closer to home—so—just maybe...

"Here we are!" announced Meg as she slowed and signaled for the off-ramp, following the big rigs down, then slowly joining the traffic in the direction of the fairgrounds. The girls were quiet now as they took in the sights of Ft. Worth: tree-lined streets; quaint shops with eye-catching displays of everything from bronze bronc sculptures to magnificent oil paintings; inviting restaurants, and grand hotels set in lush landscaping. Stately skyscrapers, many of them of shimmering glass, ensured that Ft. Worth would be a place to remember, and return to.

"Not as big as New York, but plenty big enough for me,"

stated Meg as she wound her way through traffic, careful not to miss turns or street names.

"It's nothing at all like New York. Nothing." Cass was truly impressed at this, her first trip anywhere other than close to the ranch. *Her* New York was concrete canyons and hordes of people in a rush to get somewhere. By comparison, Ft. Worth was airy, lush, and made Cass feel good.

Soon they were involved in the business of setting up their stall area in the stables, and from years of repetition, the job was done fast and looked professional. Every horse was checked closely for signs of any ill effects from their journey, the guard duty hours were settled, then everyone headed to their quarters for a well-earned rest. Tomorrow morning would come quickly, and with it the start of line classes, followed by performance classes throughout the day.

Cass's eyes darted everywhere, taking in this exciting panorama. Denton had been a great jumping-off point for her, and since then, Pat, Earl and Joshua made sure she got fine-tuned on what to expect at Ft. Worth. But they concentrated on the show, and helped her prepare her horses for the ring. Freedom now willingly took the water jumps. This had taken time and patience. Whenever she thought of this big show, her insides would flutter with excitement — or was it fear? No. She knew *real* fear, and this wasn't anything like that. Cass didn't want to let the Kileys down by doing something stupid, in or out of the ring. *That* was the kind of thing she was afraid of now.

Meals at the magnificent Chisholm Club, located in the Worthington, were to die for, and their suites offered every comfort, including a TV remote the size of a computer keyboard. They fiddled with that for a while, then Cass wandered over to the huge window which boasted breathtaking views of downtown Ft. Worth. Especially spectacular were the skyscrapers outlined in lights, their glass structure acting like mirrors for all the other lights surrounding the entire downtown area at night.

This must be a tiny corner of heaven – the mind-blowing, ever-changing visions created feelings I can't deal with. All too much – too big – too quick to disappear. I'm just waiting for this whole bubble to burst, and it's not just me being a wuss. I want to believe *in all I've seen and heard; I want to* believe *I now have a mom and dad who care, and who really love me. Funny – I do believe in* them. Sighing deeply, Cass looked up and watched a bright light coursing through the night sky. A falling star? Make a wish? Nope—just a satellite. Back to reality. Deciding it was far easier and more sensible to become a believer—even a fatalist—Cass crawled across the expanse of her king size bed.

"What a gross waste of space. I should have brought Stray up here with us—plus a few other wanderers at the stables." She snuggled between downy sheets, pulled a soft comforter up under her chin then moaned with pleasure. "Wasn't supper just the best? Imagine, steak that melts in your mouth, and tastes like it came straight from the angels, shrimps done in some sort of coconut coating—who'd ever think to do that with shrimp? And—ta-da! THE best dessert in the whole world—crème Brule, I could've eaten a dozen of -"

"*Oh shut up!*" Bri's muffled voice demanded.

"You didn't look out the window—you're missing it all."

"I've lived here all my life, remember? Haven't missed much. *Now, goodnight!*" This was final, because Bri noisily flopped around so that her back was to Cass.

"Hmmph. You're no fun."

People—all sizes and shapes—colorful shirts, jeans, exotic leather boots, Stetsons of every shape and description—and every one of them going somewhere. Not in a grim rush like New York's sidewalks, but a comfortable saunter with lots of friendly chatter. The grandstands were filled, horses were performing, with sleek bodies and rippling muscles announcing their fitness. A few balked just to make life interesting, but for the most part these were show animals, used to the noise and confusion, and ignoring it all.

Cass's first class was Junior Western Pleasure on Brandy. So many entries. Cass willed away pre-class jitters. With so many in the ring she'd be lost in the crowd. No problem. She'd just do her thing and see what happened. The PA system announced names and numbers as horses and riders trotted into the ring.

"Number 711—Cassandra Kiley on Brandy's Zip Code."

Cassandra Kiley! For the whole world to hear. I can't bear it. Leave it to me to get the number of a corner store — 7/11. She almost laughed, but quickly settled down to business. Posture. Hands. Steady gaits. Horse's head set just so. Listen to the ringmaster's commands. Be quick. Be exact in every move. Ignore the horses passing, sometimes bumping her. Pass those too slow for her own horse's gait.

The show ring didn't put Brandy off at all. She simply concentrated on looking her very best. This included covering up any goofs Cass committed, which were surprisingly few. Horse and rider circled the ring at the gait the ringmaster ordered. Cass thrilled to the graceful, unhurried progress of all fifteen competitors, even when asked to lope. So smooth. But Cass wanted the judge to see her, so tried to keep from being blocked by another horse and rider. To her this was a game and she enjoyed it enormously. To be in sync with her horse had the effect of making her feel whole, of ensuring her that she mattered. Brandy's flawless transition into the lope was merely the feel of more power being felt by Cass. Around and around they went. First clockwise then counter-clockwise, colorful clothing on the riders, silver studded saddles, bridles and breastplates on the horses.

"Line up facing the judge, please."

This was done in almost military fashion, with the horses stretching the length of the ring. A big class, and it was over. Cass wanted to stroke Brandy's sweating neck, but knew she had to wait. The judge was on his way down the line, inspecting each entry, making notes in his little book, murmuring something to each rider.

"Steady little mare, miss," he said, showing a bit of a smile.

"Thank you, sir," Cass replied quietly.

Then he was gone. That was it. Cass's insides relaxed. Brandy dared to switch her tail and snort as she gave her head a relieved toss. This time Cass did reach down to give her a well-earned pat.

"Good girl, Brandy. You did just fine."

"Number 621; number 603; number 711; number 513; number 444; step out please."

A shock jolted Cass. They'd got a ribbon—first crack! Oh, man, this is to die for. But none of this showed on her face or in her actions. She and Brandy filed toward the ringmaster and went to stand where he pointed. *Third! No – it can't be. But if I came fifth I'd be at the end of the line. I'm in the middle.*

Doing the victory lap with the other four winners, her heart nearly burst with joy. The Kileys lined the ring beside the gate, clapping and hugging, every bit as excited as Cass. With a white ribbon flowing from her bridle, Brandy loped on air so smooth were her actions as they passed through the gate.

"That wasn't so bad, was it? All that worrying about nothing. Third!" Pat reached up and pulled her down from the saddle, as Earl led Brandy away to the stables. Holding her in a bear hug, laughing, as excited as if he had won the Grand Championship.

The hoopla settled down quickly, as work began for the classes that followed. And so went the week. Their line classes in the mornings went very well, with the Rocking K winning most of the classes, ending up as Overall Champions in the Stallion, Broodmare and Yearling classes. Bri was running true to form by bringing in five firsts, two seconds and a third. Cass handled the jumping and hunter classes better than they thought she would, with only a few knock-downs. Her main faults were her slow times, but that would be worked on in the shows ahead. She did get one fifth, though, and she was over the moon about that. Matt and Sean were with Joshua and Pat in the line classes. Sean captured fourth in Junior Western Horsemanship. Totally unexpected, he earned it with a superb performance. The boy was a natural, going through his paces with no apparent effort.

Before they knew it, Friday evening had arrived, and Cass regretted allowing herself to be talked into entering the Open Jumper class. The biggie. Oh, well, why not? The huge number of entries spooked her, but, after thinking about it, she became excited. Another challenge. She looked forward to each class more than the last, loved the feeling of competing against all the gorgeous animals surrounding her. And there were some beauties, big time! Cass found out something about herself in the past month or so — if she had lots of land and money, she knew she'd take home every animal that either looked lost and pathetic, or gorgeous beyond words. Remembering her wish to become a veterinarian she groaned, knowing what emotions she'd have to deal with in that career. But she knew she was meant to do it, meant to heal others — four-legged or not, and meant to teach compassion just by being herself. Sal told her that once at Haven House. Haven House. A million light years away now, yet very much at the heart of her present situation. Cass would not forget how blessed she was — ever. Right now she wanted to do her best, like Dad said. She knew he was proud of her. Maybe someday she'd win the big one, but it really didn't matter. She and Freedom were doing their thing, and not too badly at that.

Standing outside the ring, Cass watched each performance. The horses and riders came and went, some with clean rounds, others with a few faults and still others with small disasters. This settled Cass down. She stopped thinking about herself, and watched each of her rivals, counting strides, noting which jumps the horses didn't like, what direction to approach a jump for better results; learning — always learning. Total concentration distanced her from all that was happening around her so that when her number was called, it surprised her. But it didn't rattle her. Calmly she and Freedom walked into the ring, made a small circle at the canter before approaching the first jump that set off the timer—and all else ceased to be.

Within their private world, Cass absorbed the indescribable beauty of rippling muscles gathering beneath her, stretching, lifting, briefly airborne before a controlled landing, with the proper balance already in place for the turn to the next jump. Even after such a brief experience with horses, Cass's muscles were attuned to each change of pace and direction. Breathlessly she, too, felt powerful, indestructible. A symphony, an out-of-body experience, yet always controlled. Excitement from the crowd energized her. The blending of popcorn, mustard, hot butter, Freedom's sweaty lather and hot breath were assaulting her nostrils, adding to her urgency. His breathing, like hers, became deeper and faster as they progressed around the course, sailing over the triple bars, the brush, the railroad gates and even the monstrous water jump. Freedom snorted loudly just in case someone missed his flawless effort. Then came the killer. Four jumps with just enough space between them for a horse to land, gather himself and launch into another, then another, the strain and concentration of horse and rider were breath-stopping. Cass's balance had to be perfect. Always centered, always completely one with her horse, feeling and helping his every effort, then a quiet but urgent *"Go-go-go!"* as they raced past the timer, stopping the clock. Around the end of the ring they slowed to a walk, then sedately left the ring. Freedom tossed his head vigorously, snorting and shaking the sweat and foamy lather away from his face. The resulting blobs sailed everywhere, but mostly landing all over Cass. She knew he was just showing off, and patiently scraped the glorp away from her eyes and mouth, grinning at the mess.

"Hey, girl! Awesome!" Matt was grinning from ear to ear and reached up to help her from the saddle. She slid down into his waiting arms and stayed there for an extra heartbeat. He gave her a quick squeeze before letting her go. *My heart's going to thump right out of my chest! Ohhh...that felt so good...so right.*

"Shouldn't you have stayed mounted? What if they call you back?" Meg was a bit upset. "Matt, you know better than that."

"Mom, there won't be any jump-offs except for first and second. Look at the points." Cass pointed to the board beside the chute to the ring, at the same time trying to rid her mouth of a splash of yucky horse slobber. "Anybody got some gum? A mint?" Her face screwed up in disgust.

"Here's some," offered Meg. "Now. You stay right here with us."

"Where's Dad? Did he see me? Wasn't Freedom too great?" She hugged his neck, getting in the way of Earl as he rubbed him down.

"Numbers 212, 443, 732, 414 and 711 return to the ring, please."

All motion ceased. 711. Stunned? No—shocked was more like it. This time Cass really did come close to panic—forgetting to breathe, heart hammering violently—and her old friend—a full bladder. *Oh, jeez! What'll I do? Umm...deep breaths...deep breaths...*

"Is there a jump-off?" she barely managed to croak while scrambling back onto the saddle. Matt checked the girth while Earl wiped Freedom's face and mouth.

"Go!" Meg was beside herself. "Where's Pat?"

Cass trotted into the ring and over to where the others were lining up. Freedom seemed tired; his trot was slow but still smooth, but he stopped dead as soon as he figured he was in the right spot. Then he never moved a muscle, trying to rest his hind leg by lifting the hoof onto its toe, and allowing his head to droop just a tiny bit. Cass smartened him up by gathering the reins and squeezing her legs, making him think he had to move again. Annoyed, but now fully alert long enough for the judge to present them with a huge pink rosette with wide, flowing tails embossed with gold letters — 5th place. The class all turned as one, and cantered leisurely around the ring. Freedom was the last to leave, but Cass had an awful urge to spur him on for one more victory lap, just from pure joy.

The Kileys gathered outside the ring, off to one side and out of the way of the other horses. Arms waving in victory, backs being slapped as if she'd won the World's, and all waiting to mob her. Pat took hold of the reins to lead them to the stables, while the Kiley fans crowded around, talking, laughing, whacking Cass's legs, Freedom's neck or rump, whatever they could reach. Then something happened. The horse stopped and everyone went quiet.

Cass dropped the reins and clamped a hand over her mouth, stifling a cry of alarm. Meg and Matt were beside her; Matt had his hand on Cass's knee when she dropped the reins, and he heard her muffled yelp.

"What's wrong?" Cass wouldn't answer him. She couldn't. She had turned to stone. *It's him. Tony. Again. No, no, please God, no.*

"You're pale as a ghost." Alarmed, Meg demanded, "Cass, *answer me!* What's wrong?"

"It's *him*, Mom. He's *here*."

Matt reached up, pulled Cass gently from the saddle and into his arms. She covered her face and burst into gulping sobs.

"What's she talking about, Meg? Who? What's going on?" Pat sounded frantic.

Matt held Cass close, rubbing her back, reassuring her that everything would be okay, while staring into the crowd, searching.

Lifting her head, Cass pointed to Tony. Matt turned Cass over to Meg, his face distorted with rage. He strode toward Tony.

"Who is he? What did he do?" Anger crept into Pat's voice. He turned to follow Matt.

"No, Pat! Wait! There's something you should know." Meg grabbed Pat's arm. "You *must* hear this first."

CHAPTER NINETEEN

*What's wrong with me? Am I crazy? For a second, I was so happy
to see him I wanted to run to him!* Cass ran her hands over her
face, ashamed at her reaction. At the same time, she realized
she didn't feel the heavy gloom inside her anymore. *How
come? Well, it can stay gone, 'cause I feel light as a feather! Maybe
crying like an idiot got rid of it. Maybe it was Matt's arms around
me; his head resting on mine. Nah!* Shrugging her shoulders, she
heaved a huge sigh of relief.

"Such a big sigh," murmured Meg, gently rubbing Cass's
back. "Do you want me to fill Dad in on the past or would you
like to do it?"

Stepping away and poking stray strands of hair back under
her helmet, Cass looked squarely into Meg's soft, kind eyes,
and clearly stated that she was fine now. Besides, she hadn't
told Meg everything there was to tell, and now was the time.
Her new mom and dad deserved to know what had really
happened.

"Let's sit over here." Cass indicated a picnic table stuck in a corner behind a hot dog stand. Pat put his arm around her protectively as they walked. Cass felt warmed by it, and loved. "I'll be with you in a minute. You two go sit down before somebody else grabs the table," and Meg took off into the crowd.

Scuffing through the litter strewn on the trampled grass, Cass fumed over the sloppy habits of crowds. At least four bright red trash cans stood in this area alone, yet the garbage was all over the grass. Lazy bums. Luckily the picnic table wasn't too sticky.

Cass undid the safety harness on her black velvet helmet and took it off. The stifling breeze felt good on her sweaty, matted hair. She didn't care what she looked like; never before had she felt so secure within herself. Maybe she felt comfortable with who she was; she'd heard people say that and wasn't sure what it meant.

Pat sat across from her, his big, tanned hands folded on the table, waiting for her to reveal the bits of her past she was now ready to talk about.

"I'm just going to get all of this out real quick, Dad, then you can ask whatever you want, okay?" Taking a deep breath, she continued, "but first I've gotta say, um, that, ah, being able to call you Dad and Mom, like the other kids, has made me feel, like, *real*, y'know?" He nodded, wiped his eyes, and set his black Stetson on the table. His hair was plastered down with sweat, too, the curly ends sticking out all over the place.

Taking a deep breath, Cass began her story.

"You know about where and how I lived—Mom tried. Home was a room on the fifth floor of a building whose windows were mostly boarded up, and only had running water downstairs. On our floor lived a boy, Tony Bellini, who looked after me from when I was real little right through till *that* night. He'd find food, bits of clothing, make sure I was warm, took me to school and back. He wasn't all that much older than me. He even beat up guys who were bugging me when I got older, so I never got bothered much. They were scared of him—he was big for his age. After school one night, Tony wasn't waiting for me so I started home by myself. It was real messy with dirty snow and slush, so I decided to take a shortcut down an alley, between two condemned buildings. I figured Tony wouldn't find out—he warned me not to do things like that. The dark scared me, so I ran. When I was almost at the end of the alley, a bunch of boys in Marauder gang jackets came around the corner. They blocked the alley in front of me." Her heartbeat quickened at the memory. She swallowed, and then continued. "I turned and ran back, dropping my books, screaming my head off." Her lips tightened at the memory. She fought, and won, her battle with panic.

"Cass—take it easy. It's okay. Tell me later." Pat's soft voice reached her from a far and distant place. A bottle of ice cold water appeared in front of her. When had that happened? Meg sat beside Pat, smiling encouragingly at her as she removed the caps from their bottles.

"Thanks, Mom," she murmured, and took a deep swallow. Almost too cold to bear, the icy trail down her throat scraped away all the rotten feelings that had started to invade her soul. Another gulp, a satisfied smack of tingling lips, and she was back in the past.

Looking now at those who loved her so fully and openly, Cass felt their strength.

"Well, they grabbed me and beat on me. They dragged me through a broken door into one of the old buildings. They shoved me up the bits and pieces of stairs to a place I think was the third floor. Pitch dark. Junk all over the floor. I heard hollering and laughing. I think they were drunk or high. Maybe both. When they tried to rip my clothes off, I fought and screamed as hard as I could. That got them mad. They threw me into a room, held my arms and legs, pulled my hair and started ripping my clothes. That's when I saw Tony. I thought he'd come to save me. But he had a Marauder jacket on, too, and was just leaning against the door, watching. I even screamed for him to help me. I was so scared I could hardly feel the punches anymore. There was blood—I could feel it—running down my face and chest. I felt dizzy. I'd heard about what happened to girls. Terror energized me. I fought like a maniac, then more shouting and screaming came from another room. They let go of me. I reached out to Tony, but he turned away and went to help the gang who had more girls. I can't tell you how I felt. Too terrible. Like being thrown into the garbage. I didn't know why Tony let me get beat up. I guess it got me mad enough to show him I didn't need him to save me. Somehow I ended up in a ditch full of filthy slush. I don't remember much else until I was in the hospital." Rolling the cool bottle between sweaty palms, she stared at it, murmuring, "and you know the rest." With a quivering sigh, she drained the bottle.

The only sounds came from the crowds milling around the show ring, and tents selling everything from cotton candy to bridles.

Pat picked up his hat, brushed a few flecks of dirt off it, plunked it solidly on his mussed up hair, and without a look or a word, stood and strode off to where he had last seen that tall, dark-haired boy in the bright green shirt.

Alarmed, Cass jumped up, tripped over the bench, and started after him.

"Cassandra! No!" Meg grabbed her arm. "No! Leave it to Dad."

Silently and slowly they walked to the stable area, each deep in her own thoughts.

Cass felt funny—like she'd lost weight or something. Sort of lighter. She'd been here almost a week, and hadn't noticed how beautifully all the buildings, out—buildings, tents and grandstands, had been laid out like a continuous trail of happiness. Everyone from toddlers to old folks with canes was wearing their enjoyment like neon signs. How had she missed this part of such an important fair? Had she been that blinded by her own misery that she couldn't be warmed by the happiness of those around her? What a pain she must be to everyone. Somehow, deep within, she knew she had changed today. Nobody would see it, but she could *feel* strength take root; her head was held high because — well, because it wasn't shoved into that black hole called despair — or maybe self-pity. Whatever, the cloud had lifted and she hoped it would disappear into outer space. Surely this couldn't all be because of Tony. Could it? She knew trust and honesty as far back as she could remember, and that had to be because of Tony. She knew right from wrong, and that didn't just *happen*. So, she grew up. She'd been to hell and back in less than a year. Now she felt like that same strong-minded and trusting child again. A survivor, for sure. She'd just have to fight the bad memories; "deal with it" were Dad's favorite words. Deal with it, learn from it, and forget it. *I can do that! Just watch me!*

The Kiley kids were waiting impatiently by Brandy's stall.

"Where've you been? We're starved!" Sean truly believed he was going to fall over in a faint, surrounded by goodies prepared by Kayla. These were tightly sealed inside the gigantic cooler in the tack room.

"Yep. You're right. You've all lost at least twenty pounds." Meg chortled as she sank gratefully into the cushioned patio chair next to the cooler.

Sean pouted and aimed a solid kick at the stall door. "*Owww-jeez!*" He'd forgotten he'd changed into his soft Nikes. During the laughing and teasing, Pat arrived, looking serious and a bit relieved. Cass stood quietly, not moving, waiting.

"Well?" Meg was impatient.

Looking straight at Cass, Pat related what he had discovered about Tony Bellini.

"Todd Long owns a ranch outside Celine in Grayson County. I've known that family for years. Good folks. In March he bought stock at the New York Quarter Horse Sale, and got to know a young fellow working with the sale horses. He watched him around the horses, his quiet and gentle manner, and liked what he saw. Got talking to him and found out Tony was looking for a friend, taking odd jobs around the city hoping he'd find out something about her. Eventually his story got told: how he saw a bunch of gang members grab this friend of his and shove her into an abandoned building. He followed them, alone. Inside he saw where they'd thrown their jackets, so he grabbed one, figuring he wouldn't be noticed if he wore a gang jacket. He said it was the hardest thing he'd ever done, but he had to wait till he found a chance to help her. Some other guys appeared with a couple of screaming girls and hollered for help. Tony slipped in behind them, getting in their way, hoping his friend would grab the chance to escape, if she could. He saw her sneaking out, stayed long enough to be sure the others were too busy to notice, then followed her. But she was gone. He got rid of the jacket, ran down the street to a phone box and dialed 911. There must have been a squad car close by, because he immediately heard a siren and took off. If the gang ever knew he'd squealed, well...anyhow, he had to leave town.

"He knew your love for horses, and found jobs working with them, hoping some day to find you. He says when he heard about the girl at Kileys he was scared that if it was really you, you wouldn't talk to him. He sent a note but no return address. He figured if you wanted to see him you'd find a way to get in touch. Lord knows how he came up with that, but that's what he did. When he saw you at Denton, he couldn't believe his luck. He was too scared to talk to you.

"While still in New York, Todd had Tony investigated. No police record. Good school record. So he hired him. At Denton Fair, Tony pointed Cass out to Todd, and Todd recognized us." Pat moved over beside Meg, ending with, "And that is that!"

Cass held her breath all during the telling, wanting desperately to believe what she was hearing. Her heart and soul believed every word; her mind refused to.

CHAPTER TWENTY

During this, the last day of the show, classes were still in full swing, but so were preparations for traveling home. Signs and bunting were taken down, folded and stored in special covers. Tack that wouldn't be needed that day was placed inside soft covers in tack boxes, ready for cleaning then storing for the next show.

Cass and Bri took time off to explore the midway, check out sales at the kiosks, and to relax. Their classes were later in the day; their horses were ready, their tack clean and clothes on hangers in the tack room. Strolling in companionable silence, jostled now and then by the crowd of avid horse fans, Cass puzzled over what was true...real. What should she forget about and walk away from? Which road was safest and held the least chance of yet another disaster? Why did she feel weird when Matt was near? And the one that got to her with the biggest punch was her reaction to seeing Tony. Not the stupid crying jag, but the reflex to run to him, to hold on to him like she had done for so many years, to feel whole again.

Not this time, Cass. It's not going to happen. Too much has changed to ever go back to what was. But what if what Tony said was true? He's been looking for me. So why didn't he go to the grocery store and ask? No, he couldn't do that; he thought the police were looking for him. Giving her head a quick shake she muttered, "The hell with it," and stopped to look at some silver belt buckles.

"You say something?" Bri stood beside her.

"No, not really. Just trying to clear my head of stuff that doesn't matter anymore."

"Oh." Bri stared at her, hard. "Doesn't matter anymore? Huh? Right!" Sarcasm dripped from the last word. Cass stopped what she was doing.

"What do you mean? It *doesn't* matter anymore. It's all past. I'm through being messed up with stuff that I can't change." Her voice shrilled, bordering on anger. Even Bri didn't understand. With heart hammering, palms sweaty and in tight fists, Cass shrieked, "So, tell me! What do you mean, huh? Want me to go through my entire life wearing all the shit I've been through? Thanks, Bri, thanks a bunch for caring." She whirled to stalk off, but Bri clutched her arm. Immediately the shakes and sick feeling vanished. *What's going on? I'm losing it!* Wiping her hands on her jeans, she took a deep, settling breath.

People stopped to gawk at this promise of a cat fight.

"Ah, relax, Cassy. I think you're amazing. All I meant was that 'it ain't over till it's over' and I feel there's still more to come." Bri let go Cass's arm, shrugged, and picked up a sterling silver belt buckle embossed with a web of gold. "Love it—I'm going to buy it," and she handed it to the elderly man behind the showcase.

"Bri, that costs a fortune. Besides, it's probably a fake." Also, Cass knew she had a drawer full of trophy buckles she'd won and rarely wore, all worth the moon.

"You don't sell fakes, do you, Günter?" The head of long,

pure white hair shook a definite 'no' as he gave them the benefit of his beautiful smile. "We've been buddies for years. Here. Look at this one, Cass. It has an emerald the color of your eyes."

"Just what I need, a belt buckle to match my eyes," which she rolled at Bri and gently laid the buckle on a deep-blue velvet tray. "It *is* gorgeous, though, isn't it?" Looking at Günter she asked, "Do you make these yourself?"

"*Ja*—me and two sons. Many years." His deep blue eyes could hardly be seen beneath shaggy white brows, but the pleasure of having his work praised, they shone with pride.

"Awesome," Cass breathed as she fondled the emerald buckle in wonder. "Come on, Bri, gotta go. Don't want to miss the last big gathering of the show."

"I'll catch up. I want to buy this gold web one. It has *me* written all over it."

Cass laughed, shook her head and wandered toward the next vendor's stall. An unusual, tooled leather purse caught her eye. She reached for it just as a grating female voice shouted Bri's name. Cass turned, curious.

"Hey, ol' buddy—what's happenin'?" Jet black hair held securely by one long braid down her back, and boobs she must have found at Targets, jerked her thumb in the general direction of Cass.

"Hello, Tina." Obviously Bri didn't consider herself an 'ol' buddy'.

"Hey—is *this* the gutter rat your folks dragged home? What's she like? Is she dirty? Does she talk trashy, y'know, stuff like that?" All this rattled from over-painted lips like bullets from an Uzi.

"*Tina!*" Bri was dumbfounded, her mouth agape.

Cass, on the other hand, was all business. So, *that's what the townies think of me. Well I've got a flash for them; just wait till school starts.* Feeling her anger building to the flashpoint, she took a couple of deep breaths, then strode back to stand face-to-face with Tina. This was New York-type stuff that she could deal with in a heartbeat.

Bri grabbed her arm. "Cassy, no. She's not worth it."

"Not worth it? *Not worth it?*" screamed Tina. "Just who in hell do you think you are anyway, Miss Rich Bitch? Million dollar horses and now your very own slum skunk to clean up!"

That was too much for Bri. She aimed a wicked shot at Tina's face. Cass deflected it and held onto Bri's shaking fist.

In a controlled, low, and deadly voice, Cass began.

"Yes, Tina, I'm the product of a New York slum. Most of New York is beautiful. But some of it shouldn't even exist. It's beyond hell." Fighting to maintain her control, Cass continued. Tina stared in fascination—was this girl going to kill her or talk her to death?

"What's your last name, Tina?"

"Bellingham." The once strident voice had become wary.

"Ah! So you know who your father is. You're lucky, because I don't." Cass dared her to make something of this bit of information. Tina remained mute. Wise move.

"We'll be at the same school this fall. I will be the new kid on the block. So to make things a whole lot easier on you and your snotty friends, here's the dirt." Cass took one step closer to Tina, both hands clenched by her sides. Bri had turned into stone. "Home was a filthy hole five floors up, inside an abandoned building. I had to lie, cheat and fight to get to school. I spent my time trying to find food, trying to stay hidden from street gangs. Most girls my age, and younger, are selling themselves so they can eat. No hope. No dreams. No one cares about them. Soon they'll know it's not going to get any better. Then come the drugs. Yeah, Tina, that's *their* American Dream!" Cass reached out and grabbed the front of Tina's blouse. Tina gasped in fear. "*Are you listening, Miss Bellingham, spoiled brat of the Bellinghams?*"

Tina nodded slowly, and tried to back away. But a crowd had gathered. A silent crowd. This was no ordinary cat fight.

"Okay. I got lucky. I got beaten up so bad I ended up in hospital. That's the first time I knew that soap made suds and smelled good. That's the first time my hair got shampooed. First real meal, which I threw up. I wasn't used to more than a couple of mouthfuls of food at a time. Was I ashamed? No. Was I angry? No. I was determined to get the hell away from the city and into a place with green grass and fresh air. Then I'd find a job. Then I'd study all night every night. Then I'd go to university. I refused to become a gutter rat. So, this is a warning to you and everyone like you. Don't ever, ever call me that again. You got off easy this time, and that's because of the most wonderful family on this planet. They're good, caring and patient human beings who have made me who I am. They gave me life, in the truest sense of the word, and I'll do whatever it takes to make them proud of me. I will not shame them by rearranging your face." She let go of Tina's blouse with a little shove. "Can you say the same? I don't think so — all you know is how to get your own way. I pity your poor parents with a selfish shit like you for a daughter."

Turning away, Cass fired one last shot, this time a bit louder and a lot firmer. "Don't give me or my family any trouble, you hear me?" She walked away to the sound of silence.

"Hey! Where ya been?" Matt hurried to catch up with her, unaware of the scene in front of the jewelers — and half of Ft. Worth's horsy set.

Cass walked tall, at peace with herself and knowing exactly who she was. She had made a statement for the world to hear, and she had no regrets.

"Wandering around. This is totally great. You should see the belt buckle Bri's buying back there."

"*Another* one? I bet it's from old Günter, right?" He slung his arm across her shoulders. Cass was glad he couldn't hear the thumping of her heart.

"You got it." *Appear normal, Cass. Don't let him know your knees have turned to jelly.*

As they neared the tent, Cass searched the groups enjoying idle chatter outside. There he was. Tony, with Todd and their crew. His eyes met hers, lit up, and the familiar movie star smile spread across his face as he hurried toward them. Cass stopped dead in her tracks, heart thudding, breath short. *Never forget, Cassy- — betrayal! Oh, give it up, Cass. Let it go. NOW.*

"Jeez!" Matt grated out with venom and strode up to Tony, landing a well-aimed sucker punch. Tony spun around, staggered, a look of utter disbelief on his face.

"Matt! No!" Cass looked over at Tony who was rubbing his jaw.

"That felt good — I'll keep this jerk away from you. Are you okay, Cassy?" She didn't know whether to laugh or cry.

"That was dirty, Matt. No fair. You're so wrong about him."

Matt was rubbing his knuckles, a look of grim satisfaction on his face. He was no fighter, but he had hated this guy who had hurt Cass ever since she arrived at the ranch. Cass understood his need to defend her, so she put her arms around him and told him she was okay, that Tony wouldn't hurt her. A quick kiss on his cheek and she told him to go. But he held her close just long enough for a gentle kiss on her lips, which held promises for all the good tomorrows. Another quick peck on the cheek and he was gone.

Ohmygod! What's happening to me? She took a deep breath to settle down, then went to see to Tony. As she walked over to him, she thought, *that was a shocker — I loved it. I love Matt. My very first real kiss. I could fly to the moon...back to earth, Cass. You're in a mess here.*

"Tony, I'm so sorry." He rubbed his jaw.

"Like being back in the old neighborhood," he chuckled.

"That was Matt. He wasn't there when Dad told us your side

166

of the story." Cass chewed the inside of her cheek as she waited for Tony to talk to her. Matt's timing stunk.

"Not your fault, Punkin." He ran his fingers through his mop of blue-black curls then put both hands on her shoulders. Those eyes — oh, those eyes. *Why did all this have to happen? So many people; so much hurt and fear.* Blinking to break that line of thought, Cass looked away, reminding herself of the many great things that had come her way because of that brutal night in New York, a lifetime ago. Her head, heart, soul all felt different now. *Is this what 'normal' means?* Tony wanted to prove his worth, he had told Dad. Would that make him a good person, a "normal person"?

She knew he had a long way to go to earn *her* trust again.

They stared at each other for an eternity then, without a word needing to be spoken, hand-in-hand, they entered the tent, grabbed plates, piled on the food and joined the Kileys. Cass knew she looked different by the way each of the family tried not to let her catch them staring at her, then Tony. She sure *felt* different.

Was it because of Matt, and her growing love for him, or Tony because of all he had been to her since forever?

Before her last class, the whole clan clustered around her, offering last minute instructions, warning of rumors that the water jump now had a hedge in front of it. This would have gone on until she entered the ring, so Cass held up her hands for them to cool it.

"I have something to say." She cleared her throat.

"It'd better be fast — I've got to go you-know-where." Sean and his bladder.

"It will be." Looking at each of them with a love she could never put into words, she began to speak, soft and low. "We all know the whole story now — at least the important bits — and I can tell you that, as of right now, I feel whole, entirely different. Life doesn't get any better." Blinking back a tear, she lowered her head before continuing in words that trembled with an inner emotion that threatened to strike her dumb. *Please, God, help me through this. Help me find the right words.* With that little prayer safely in her heart, she was able to continue.

"Thank you, from the bottom of my heart, um, for, ah, giving me my life. I swear that you'll never, ever be sorry." Cass paused. "Somehow, Tony completes me. He's been the only family I've ever known. I, ah, don't know why, after...well, I just want to say thanks—all of you. I love you so much..." Her words faded to a whisper as she escaped into Freedom's stall to bury her face in his shiny mane. Tears of joy trickled down his warm, familiar neck, while she savored his distinctive barn smell.

"Leave her," Meg held onto Bri's arm as she made to follow. "She needs to be alone for a few minutes." Sniffing, she swiped at her eyes, then ordered everyone to get the horses tacked up and over to the ring. Except Matt. Meg looked back and saw her son holding her new daughter tight, comforting her, and laughing quietly.

"Hmmm," Meg muttered to herself. "This could get a bit dicey."

The laughter increased, and she knew she'd been overheard.

"Damn!"

Horses, riders, owners, friends and eager enthusiasts gathered at ringside, staying out of the way of the competitors as they entered and left the ring. An unusually large class of fifteen registered Paint jumpers milled around, waiting their turn to compete. This particular event was a real crowd pleaser. And, once again, Cass jumped last.

Mounted on Freedom, she walked him around the smaller warm-up ring, then pushed him into a slow canter, then back to a walk, keeping his muscles loose and his attention keen.

Cass forced herself to focus on the job ahead. She soared on a super high, all because of the love for her family, for Matt, and the beginnings of a renewed faith in Tony.

"Number 711, Cassandra Kiley on Freedom" boomed the P.A. system.

Cass's heart lurched. Her focus snapped to attention. All business now, they trotted to the gate, passing well-wishers and family without seeing or hearing them. Her heart pounded in her ears. Heaving a couple of deep breaths to steady her pounding heart, she had Freedom canter slowly in a small circle before surging past the timer and into the first jump. Cass merged, body and soul, with the fabulous beast she was astride, as they soared over the striped poles. Muscles bunched, stretched, relaxed and reached out for two strides before rising again, a gleaming, well-oiled machine. And on it went, Cass encased in her bubble of total concentration, guiding, urging, alert, thinking two steps ahead of their next move. No hedge had been added at the water jump, but a single white pole lay on the far edge of the stretch of water. The jump looked much wider than any they had ever attempted before. *Just stay steady, Cass, don't let him sense you're uptight.* Tasting blood, she knew she'd bitten her tongue.

Turning to approach the water, Freedom's ears snapped forward so they almost touched at the tips, snapped back, then forward again—never missing a beat.

"Atta boy, go, go –*hup!*" Cass's chest and arms moved up the sweat-lathered neck, rising up and forward out of the saddle, and flew with him up, over, down and on toward the triple bars. The far off clamor and cheering of the crowd seeped into her bubble, driving a timely and vital surge of energy through her strained and tired body.

"One more, Free, one more!" Encouraging him as much as herself, they headed for the final jump—the railroad gate flanked by banks of bright flowers on either side of the approach. The knowing steed somehow sensed that this was it. After the last jump he knew they ran full tilt between two white posts. He charged passed the flowers, cleared the gate by at least a foot, flattened his ears and stretched his neck as he charged through the timer's beam.

The roar from the crowd was deafening. Cass acknowledged them with a nod and a grin. She slapped Freedom joyfully on his lathered neck. His head was high and eyes glistening as he trotted proudly through the path opened up by those watching at the gate. A clean round, but was it fast enough? Cass couldn't focus on the faces; sweat ran into her eyes, stinging and causing a frantic check of pockets for a tissue. Swiping her dripping nose, a private chuckle escaped dry lips.

Hey, girl – you done right some good. At this point she realized that she had just experienced the best fun ever, and couldn't wait to tell the gang.

Off to one side, Cass saw the Rocking K gang and rode up to them. They were laughing and talking all at once. Freedom danced like a frisky colt till Earl caught him by the bridle.

"Numbers 732, 212, 711, 302 and 443 return to the ring, please!"

Cass stared at the loudspeaker above her head, hoping it would reel off the numbers once more, because she didn't believe it. 711. Couldn't be!

Earl still had hold of the bridle and quickly turned Freedom and ran with him back to the ring yelling, "Watch it! 'Scuse us! Stand back!" all the way. Finally in the ring, he turned them loose to follow the other horses, and to stand where the ringmaster pointed. Cass almost exploded with excitement, still on a huge high, still full of wonder that her dreams had become reality. Now the cheers of the crowd assaulted her ears: such beautiful music. The buttery popcorn and fries filled her nostrils, making her stomach growl. This exercise sure worked up an appetite. She mused about the months of effort that had gone into preparing for this show. Plus months of heartache and uncertainty.

Who would have thought I'd end up here, doing this, less than a year ago? That I'd be so filled with pride and love for the sport, that I'd be a "natural," as Dad predicted. How can a cold, frightened, hardened street kid learn what caring, love, and all that stuff really means? Yeah. I know. Right place – right time – and the Kiley family.

Clearing her head by closing her eyes for a few moments, she was ready to do and say the proper things when presented with the precious white ribbon. The loudspeaker had been right.

Within minutes they were trotting swiftly out of the ring with the ribbon snapping against Freedom's neck. Third! Unbelievable!

Again Earl whisked her off to one side, but farther away this time. The ranch gang milled around near an enormous live oak, and each of the Kileys waved short, slim batons or sticks.

Why are they way over there?

"What's going on?" she asked Earl, "and what's with the sticks?"

She slid from the saddle, her legs a little shaky from all the stress, hugged Freedom around the neck, and drank in the heady scent of a hard working, healthy horse, before Earl led him away.

Cass turned to the family. All she could say was, "Wow!" and threw her arms in the air, clutching the long white rosette she'd snatched off the bridle.

"This is awesome. Imagine how I'll feel if I ever win – I'll explode!" Something behind her caught her eye. Tony stood shyly at the edge of a group of onlookers, so proud she thought he'd burst.

"Tony! You're here. Did you see it?" He ran the short distance between them, grabbed her and swung her around.

Pulling him by the hand, they joined the family.

"Hey, Tony." That was Sean and Bri in unison, making Tony feel welcome.

"How's it going, Tony? Great ride, eh?" Pat slapped his shoulder. He'd take his time figuring out what this guy was really after — then he'd make up his mind about how much the Kileys would have to do with him in the future. In the meantime — he'd relax.

Matt stood like a stone, looking very uncomfortable, until Tony reached out to shake his hand. "Want to see my bruise? Coloring up nicely."

They both grinned.

"Cassy, girl, in our hearts you *have* won," boomed Pat as he walked toward her. They all crowded around and handed her their sticks. She accepted them with a sidelong glance at Matt, who just shrugged and grinned. She shivered, seeing that awesome smile.

What am I supposed to do with these things? It seems so important to them.

"Okay, you guys — what's going on? I've won? Won what? Are you all nuts?" They broke out laughing, then Meg held out an empty clay pot.

Someone help me out here...this is making me crazy...

"This urn was made at the ranch, from the soil of the ranch, by Dad's mother, your grandmother Maureen. Here. Put the branches in it. Keep them forever." Mom's lips trembled.

Branches! Not sticks — branches. From each member of the family. Of course — the Family Tree.

"Cass?" murmured Dad.

Tearing her gaze from the urn, which she had hugged to her chest, she saw each of them holding onto the edge of a glass-and-oak framed picture. She blinked in the sun's glare, moving in for a closer look.

"Look!" Sean couldn't stand it any longer and was pointing to something in the picture. No. Not a picture. A tree. The gnarled but stately oak tree that hung so proudly in the office at home.

"*LOOK!*" Sean was beside himself with excitement.

Then she saw it. A brand new branch, *her* branch, grew from the trunk of the Kiley Family Tree. Cass traced it with a trembling finger. *And I thought life couldn't get any better. But I don't understand. It's...it's all so...oh, God, what has happened to Your little gutter girl?*

"Cass? You okay?"

Nodding slowly, Cass looked up at her new dad as if for the first time.

My father...my dad. When will my heart let me believe? How do I recognize love? Trust? Have faith, Cass. Patience and faith.

Dad was showing her the new Family Tree.

"My grandmother's name—Maureen. I hope you don't mind." Dad put his arm gently around her as she softly read her name aloud.

"Cassandra Maureen Kiley."

Home at last...

Printed in the United States
55110LVS00002B/1-66

9 781413 790993